Dangerous Double-Jeu

Pauline Walters

Contents

To all the good girls who sit when it fits. I got you.

Contents Warning

This book contains dark themes, <u>mostly</u> off pages with no detailed description, but mentioned.
Death and murder (on page/off page), violence (descriptive as well as non descriptive), assault, abduction, pedophilia (mention), underaged girls brothel (no description of SA), SA against teenage girls, torture against women (some on pages) and underage girls, castration (off page) mentions of rape, PTSD, body mutilation.

Reader discretion is strongly advised.
It explores morally complex characters and may not be suitable for all readers.
Also, it's kinky.

Prologue

Night had long fallen on Dublin, and despite the recent murders, people were still outside taking advantage of the last "sunny" days of summer. A dark figure hid, observing this little world, waiting for her target to leave his imposing-look-at-me mansion, clueless of the destiny awaiting him outside. The moon broke from behind the clouds, gently illuminating the figure waiting to fulfil her revenge.

Their revenge.

Just kidding, she just loved to kill.

Eve stood, arms folded over her stomach, gaze locked on the building's door. Her long braid floated slightly in the wind.

"Finally" she muttered, watching the door open on a man built like a gorilla, looking suspiciously around, before stepping aside to let the target pass. *Senator Andrews.* Well-respected by the Irish, he had notably created harsh punishments for those guilty of sexual crimes, making it look as no pity would be applied to guilty offenders. Too bad he wasn't respecting his own rules.

The young woman moved, running to follow them. Reaching her motorbike, Eve accelerated as the men in the car took off. The possible cameras didn't worry her too much. She made sure the plate number she used for her night hobbies did not exist in the police files.

The car and its tail headed east, leaving the hustle and bustle of the fancy city centre, to the so-called "Irishtown" neighbourhood. It was supposed to be one of the most secure in the city, maybe even the most secure, many people moved there after the war. Even she did, which was quite ironic, considering her favourite hobby and day job.

At the end of the neighbourhood, the car stopped in front of a somewhat dilapidated building. The edifice made of bricks seemed more abandoned than anything else. Senator Andrews got out of his Mercedes and walked toward the entrance, surrounded by his two gorillas.

Eve frowned. *There shouldn't still be buildings like this in this corner of the city.* If her information was accurate, what was behind this façade was not what the neighbours, and herself, had signed up for when moving in.

Finally finding an accessible window, she climbed up to the ledge, looking into a room decorated with large black curtains hanging on the walls, more than dubious elements all over the place. A large wooden table sat in a corner of the room, with ties. These people were such a cliché when it came to sadism it was almost sad.

The door opened in a clatter and Eve quickly pulled herself up, hiding behind the window posts. A man pulled his victim behind him, a young woman — probably closer to her teenage years than actual womanhood — eyes widening, pleading with the man. Her tiny figure too weak to resist his strength.

Eve furrowed her eyebrows, the man's face was familiar, but who? She tried to get her memory working, imagining those big ugly eyebrows, and that skin studded with freckles somewhere in her past, but she couldn't.

Meh, he will die anyway. The man pulled the girl towards the wooden table, trying to avoid her kicks.

Deciding it was time to act, Eve clung to a ledge, kicking the window as hard as she could, smashing it to pieces. She landed delicately in the room, the crunch of glass under her boots, rushing towards the man still in a state of surprise, his flaccid penis hanging miserably. Throwing her right arm forward, she sent a flash of metal straight into the man's throat. The teenager opened her mouth but forced herself to shut up when Eve beckoned her not to scream. She looked back at the man dying on the ground, blood flowing from his open throat, a smile on her face.

"What's your name?" Eve turned back to the girl.

"Ellen..."

"Don't look at him Ellen. I'm going to check the rest of the building. I want you to stay here, call the police and they'll come and get you to take you home, okay?"

Ellen nodded, shivering. "What if they think I did it?"

Eve's smile widened. "Don't worry, they won't suspect you."

She walked to the door, towards the screams.

Time to have some fun!.

Chapter 1

Detective Mark

11 bodies, all naked and bloody men. Most well-known citizens. Detective Mark shook his head, he could see it coming from here. *This is going to be such a scandal.* Senators, CEOs, even a mayor; all murdered while having a good time in a somewhat special brothel. If he hadn't been the one on duty, he'd be laughing right now. Too bad this was now his problem.

The Detective sighed, looking at the horde of journalist standing just a few feet from him and the building. He had immediately spotted the famous news anchor from TV1, gesticulating, showing with a furious hand the tall dark structure, now full of bodies. Mark's colleagues used the yellow tape, but since the war, the barrier didn't really mean anything anymore and this journalist was as always way too close for Mark's taste. In the good old days, he would have at least been allowed to beat him up.

He mumbled while foraging through the pockets of his trench, hoping he had one of his favourite chocolate bars left.

All those men slaughtered in cold blood, and no freaking clues. Just one blood-thirsty killer.

"No, you can't pass Sir...!!"

The Detective raised his head. *No chocolate, and now Cyrus freaking McRory.*

Chapter 2

Cyrus

Cyrus's brows knitted together, teeth clenched, eyes blazing with anger. Each step was powerful and he could already see Detective Mark starting to crumble a bit, watching him move closer with a pained smirk on his face.

Cyrus held back a scoff when Zorfied sniggered behind him.

Cyrus halted mid-stride, turning his gaze locked onto the poor policeman behind them who dared to comment. With a slight raise of his brow and a measured pause, Cyrus addressed the officer, his voice flat but deep. "I am Cyrus McRory, and I do what I want." He waited a few seconds, watching the man in front of him deflate, his fair skin even paler, eyes rounding with a slight touch of fear. "Why don't you put the journalists back in their place instead?"

With little surprise, Mark's colleague stepped back, heading to the journalists, before Cyrus stopped him.

"And if they don't want to move, tell them I'll send Zorf."

The bleached blond with obsidian eyes and a sarcastic smile perpetually living on his lips smiled at the reporters. Ian next to him, just rolled his eyes.

The policeman on duty could only nod his head, catching Mark's eyes, but to Cyrus's satisfaction, the detective just waved his hand. He probably had other priorities right now. Mark was one of those cops who didn't really "care" about him and his extra activities. They even kind of liked each other. After all they had been to high school together, and much later collaborated during the war. Besides, Cyrus was always generous with people who helped him, and who helped others, he was genuinely concerned about his country and his people. So was Mark.

And Mark was not dumb. He had seen enough of what happened to anyone who went in the way of Cyrus as early as intermediate school.

"Cyrus." Mark nodded, hands still in pockets, probably hoping it would at least give him an air of self-confidence.

"Mark, details, now," Cyrus growled. Politeness had never been his strong point.

He stood motionless, towering over the detective in front of him, holding back a laugh as Mark scratched his head nervously. Silence grew heavy, and Cyrus could feel Zorf's impatience, his friend taping his foot on the concrete. They knew it was bad, and Mark's reaction and silence was only confirming this. Cyrus pinched his brow, not sure why the detective was so scared to talk. It's not as if he was personally responsible for the mess now, was he?

Cyrus tried not to let a satisfied smile stretch across his face; there was one explanation for Mark's fear right now. Irishtown, the neighbourhood they were standing in right now, was also called Cyrustown. Cyrus controlled everything around here: who worked, who lived, who paid, who made trouble. And if you were making trouble, you were usually nowhere to be seen soon after.

"Tell me," Cyrus said finally.

Mark swallowed hard. "That was kind of brothel..." Mark muttered, looking like a little boy guilty of stealing sweets.

Cyrus's eyes narrowed, a flicker of anger passing through them. His arms tightened across his chest, muscles tense. He gave a curt nod, barely more than a tilt of his head.

"But worse..."

He could feel the fury flashing across his face. This time his eyebrows were so furrowed they looked like one on his forehead.

"Theyreallunderage."

There was no need for yelling. Cyrus looked up at the dark and decrepit building, aware of Mark watching him, waiting for his reaction.

Cyrus stood still, eyes fixed on the bricks building, lips pressed into a thin line. His fingers drummed an unknown rhythm against his thigh, hinting at some form of chaos hidden under his calm appearance.

"Can we go in?" Cyrus asked without giving Mark a look.

At the lack of answer, he turned his head back towards the detective, now grimacing, as if pulled by two distinct forces. The fear of Cyrus, and the fear of his boss.

Mark exhaled, louder than necessary, walking toward the entrance, the others close behind. As usual, the first was the winner.

"Yeah... the guys finished taking stock. We need to take away the girls now."

"How many?"

"22."

Cyrus and his companion's eyes widened, the three of them now staring at Mark.

"Yep, and they're almost all kids, most between 12 and 16. The oldest is 18. Told us she had been there for 5 years... We did a quick search. Turns out they're all missing kids from the war. Remember those families trying to survive?"

Cyrus nodded.

"Looks like they sold their offspring to the Reseau."

The Reseau....

A scandal broke out when the war was close to an end. Among many other atrocities, authorities learned some desperate families had given their kids to the biggest prostitution network in Ireland, the infamous Reseau. Cyrus, Ian, and Zorfield were unofficially charged with the task of deep cleaning the existing mess. It mostly went unnoticed, the streets were still filled with blood, and at the time, no one wanted to ask questions.

They had a lot of fun.

"I thought we cleared those." Ian's soft voice hung in the air.

"Same here." Mark grunted, exchanging a look with Cyrus before entering the building.

They all did things during the war they never wanted to think about, but cleaning the Reseau wasn't something any of them regretted.

And now this? It didn't sound good. Cyrus couldn't believe something so big had passed right under his nose. He thought he was finally in control of everything in this part of the city. He made sure of it, he worked hard for it. He killed for it. Heads were going to roll, and they needed to roll fast.

Inside the building, two dislocated bodies lay on the beautiful Persian carpet, naked. Dried blood puddled under their bodies, their flaccid dicks hanging out.

"We assume they tried to flee from the upstairs rooms." Mark pointed to two doors, looking out onto the stairs. "Apparently the killer started on the right side of the building, climbing up to a window, like a fucking cat. Then cleared her way through the corridors. These men must have heard screaming and got scared." Mark took a deep breath, "She caught up with them here in the entrance."

"She?" Ian looked confused.

"Yes, apparently a woman did this," Mark added.

"On her own?" Ian asked.

"Yep."

Ian looked up at the stairwell, dreading the spectacle awaiting them.

"Can we talk to the girls?" Cyrus asked.

Mark looked at him. "I can't let you do that Cyrus, I might get in trouble and you know it." There was only so much he could allow, even Cyrus knew that, but he was not ready to give up.

"This is my neighbourhood. It's up to me to take care of it."

"But this is murder. It is up to the police to deal with them." Mark sighed, his face showing he didn't believe one word of what he just said.

Cyrus burst out laughing. "It's not our lady killer I want to find. It's all the customers of this damn brothel. Let's clear the fucking Reseau once and for all. We worked too hard to let his happen again."

Mark shook his head, and when Cyrus turned to his friends, Zorf and Ian were nodding in approval. The smirk on Zorf's thin lips, showcasing how excited he was about the idea. Cyrus turned back to Mark, who was looking around. "She killed Senator Andrew," murmuring, he leaned closer to Cyrus. "Given what she did to him, I bet he was the one she wanted. She just decided to change her plans when she saw the other vermin hanging around here."

Zorfield chuckled. "Senator Andrews? You can't be serious? "

"Unfortunately, yes." Mark sighed. "Apparently he had some inclinations for tied teenage girls."

Cyrus let out a light chuckle. "I knew there was a reason you look like you wished you didn't take the call."

Senator Andrews, well-respected by the entire island, had acted at the end of the war as a caring politician, enabling rougher laws for anyone guilty of sexual crimes, even condemning with severity any participation in the Reseau.

Oh the irony.

Murmurs and sniffles broke the silence as a small troop of women descended from the upper floor. Fragile, pale, and covered in bruises and marks, they looked even younger than they were. Barely teenagers, some holding hands, their knuckles whitening under the pressure. One girl saw the two bodies on the floor and started laughing hysterically, causing a break in the armada of female policemen and paramedics cautiously surrounding them. A cop stepped aside to cater and comfort the girl, now breaking down in tears.

Cyrus's fists trembled at his sides, trying to hold back from punching something or someone. "Let me talk to them. I want to know every client they've dealt with."

"And what will you do to them, Cyrus? Will you kill them?" Unlike Cyrus, Mark had lowered his voice, conscious of the many ears in the room. "We're not at war anymore." He shook his head, placing his hand on Cyrus's shoulder. "You do know Erik is getting replaced by Cragnum, right? And everyone at the station is on edge because of the other murders."

Cyrus scoffed. "Let me take care of my own ass Mark. I'm sure you and I can work this out."

A girl broke away from the group, walking quickly towards the men, her long blond hair falling on her shoulders, wrapped in a blanket, trying to hide the outfit underneath.

"Ellen! Come back here!" A female police officer followed behind.

"Are you going to stop her?" Ellen stood tall, and despite her weaken features her face was showing the fight she still had in her. "Even though she is the one who saved us!" The other girls paused, turning to the discussion.

"She committed horrific murders, Miss... it's my job," Mark said with waning conviction.

"Come and spend one night with us in this place, and you will understand what horrific means." The girl now held an air of disgust, her mouth twisted while her hands clenched over and over on the blanket. "What these men were doing to us, wasn't it your job to stop them? You want to look for our... our saviour instead of finding the sons of bitches allowing THIS! Do you know how many politicians have fucked me during my five months here?? How many policemen?? Do you think they were doing their JOB then?" Ellen screamed, setting off the tears of several behind her.

Cyrus pivoted on his heel, a smug smile tugging at the corners of his lips as his eyes locked onto Mark's. Mark's jaw clenched, and he averted his look to answer to the young girl. "I have to do my job, but if it makes you feel any better, we don't have any clues... and strangely, none of you remember her face, nor her voice, and oh surprise, nothing about her allure in general."

Ellen stiffened. "Half of her face was covered by a mask, and we were busy, you know, having dicks in our ass and stuff" The policewoman pulled her by the arm bringing her back to the rest of the group, finally moving the survivors out.

"Useless witnesses, inspector?" Cyrus snickered.

"Fine, I'll get you up to speed, but then you leave before Erik or the Duo arrive. They don't like you meddling in our investigations."

"Not my problem."

Mark sighed, but bowed. "Okay, here's the story. 11 dead, most by haemorrhage, throats sliced by some metal object. The girls told us about some kind of "star" attached to a wire, which the killer swung in all directions, and apparently, she aims damn well. The first to be killed was in the company of the girl there, Ellen, in a charming room decorated with taste... I'll send you pictures if that helps. Then it looks like she went out, cleaned the other rooms, before spending some one-on-one time with Andrews."

"What did she do to him?" Ian asked, a glimmer of curiosity in his eyes.

Mark scoffed. "Not nice things, I'll tell you that." He shook his head. "She sliced off his dick. The ME thinks he was still alive."

Zorfield bust out laughing before Ian gave him a light kick.

"That's all?" Cyrus asked.

"I told you, we have almost nothing!" Mark grumbled, frustrated. "No prints yet, she had gloves, no hair or whatever. All we could get from the girls was that she was dressed in leather, had a black mask covering the top of her face, moved fast, and had a soft voice. Like I said, we don't have anything!"

"Indeed, it's meagre... I guess they don't remember her hair, her eyes, her mouth...??" Cyrus asked, his voice full of sarcasm, it seemed the girls would be no help finding the lady killer, but his little finger told him they would be quite talkative about their past customers.

"We'll leave you to it Mark." Cyrus nodded. "We've got work to do, going to try to find out more about who was holding this thing."

"Yeah, and I'm going to have to investigate this girl... Cyrus, remember the July murder?"

Cyrus frowned. "You mean the Lovish date that turned really bad?" He didn't pay much attention, but the poor girl had invited a guy she found on the latest dating app and things turned ugly. Her raped body showed evidence of torture.

"Yeah, that one." Mark stopped, looking over his shoulder. "We have another one, almost in all points similar, but the big heads don't think it's the same killer, so they have different teams working the cases. I think it's the same guy, and the Duo agrees."

"Are they working both?" Cyrus asked.

"Andy and Bonnie are on the first one. I am on the recent, for now. We're communicating and comparing, but we were told to stick to a single killer." He paused, looking at Cyrus. "Rumour is, maybe someone would like us to pin it on you, or at least get you in trouble."

Cyrus's brows knitted together. *Why? How?*

"Looks like you knew both girls." Mark shrugged.

Cyrus clicked his tongue. *Now that is an unfortunate coincidence.* Though to be fair, he knew many people, especially women. And Ireland was not that big. *Come on!* The coroner's troupes were coming in, signalling his time was almost up with Mark.

"What's their names?" *Not that he would remember a one-night stand.*

"Roisin Garvin and Mary Murphy."

Brows formed a V on Cyrus's forehead. He knew MANY Roisins and Marys. Those must be some of the most common first names in this country.

"You've had them both." Ian sighed, rolling his eyes.

"I did?"

Ian exhaled, his head shaking from left to right in disapproval, while Zorfield chuckled behind his back. Ignoring his friends, Ian turned towards Mark.

"I can find out the dates Cyrus met the girls if that will help? And probably some alibi too, for the nights of the murders."

Cyrus knew Ian had been keeping track of his endeavours, hoping it would come in handy one day, looked like he was right.

I swear I'm never making fun of his attention to detail again.

"Well, it's not like having you telling us Cyrus was hanging out with both of you at home is gonna help his case much. You're not that credible." Mark shrugged. "No offence."

Ian opened his mouth, ready to protest—

"Heyyy!" Zorfield walked over, hands on his hips, his obsidian eyes shining with some crazy light. "Offence taken! I'm not credible, but Ian is great!"

"Thanks babe," Ian sighed, while Cyrus tried to hold back a laugh before getting back to his concerned face.

"Well, that's all great. We didn't even know there was a second one." Cyrus glanced at Ian, who nodded his head.

"Like I said... Erik's time is coming to an end." Mark sighed. "So... about those murders." He leaned his head in the direction of the bloody puddle on the floor, the bodies now taken by the coroner. "I have to send my daughters to college next year..."

Cyrus's lips curled into a slow, calculated smile, his eyes narrowing with mischief. As usual, he would get what he came for. "I want all the reports, depositions, and clues you're going to get. I don't care about the lady killer; I want the clients and managers of the brothel. Do that, and you won't pay a cent for your kids' time at uni."

Mark hesitated before finally shaking his head. "Okay, deal."

Cyrus scratched his chin. "Let's add those two last murders on to the list as well, will you?"

Ian glanced at Cyrus. "Are you sure this is a great idea Cyr'? If you are a suspect, that's just gonna attract attention to us. We don't need that."

"If I can add." Mark cleared his throat, motioning them toward the door. "Those files might be hard to get to you."

"What do you mean?" Ian eyed him.

"We are not supposed to take anything out of the station, we are being watched about what we're doing and finding. Cragnum decided he would be the one getting the merit for it, something about wanting to start as a strong Commander, finding a serial killer and stuff. And because anyone with a tad of neurones knows you have many informants in the police..."

Mark stepped out of the building after his short speech, taking a deep breath, his eyes looking around suspiciously, groaning when he spotted something outside. Cyrus followed his look, frowning at the cameras.

"Fine, I guess I will have to ask Erik himself." Cyrus smiled.

"Good luck with that. Cragnum is on his back. I am personally going to focus on those." Mark shoved his hand around, designing the crappy building.

"That's a dead-end Mark." Ian tilted his head.

"Why is that?"

"Did you hear Ellen? 'The Saviour.' In spite of herself, she has just given her name to this killer. She saved dozens of young girls from the atrocities that high ranked men committed. She's going to attract a whole bunch of followers. No one will help you; no one will testify. By choosing this 'branch' if I may say so, she has ensured her own safety. I mean, look, even Cyrus isn't that interested in finding her."

"That's a fair point." Cyrus looked at Mark, eyebrows raised. Ian could have been the best profiler in Great Britain if it weren't for his relationship with the famous gang leader.

Mark shook his head. "Do you really think that?"

"Of course." Ian stopped, no doubt pondering what he found inside. "I would even say she's killed before, but probably managed to do it with discretion. I'm sure if we searched hard enough, we could track her." He shook his head. "But here her anonymity is dead. So, there are only two outcomes. Either she will become more violent, because she will feel protected; or she'll calm down and let things blow over. But given how she seems to appreciate the killing, I doubt it."

DANGEROUS DOUBLE-JEU

17

Chapter 3

Eve

"Both Senator Andrews and Colm Lynch the mayor of Kilkenny have been found along with nine other dead bodies, murdered in grisly circumstances..." Eve turned off the television, she had seen enough.

Not bad kid, you killed your first politicians!

It's all the news was talking about, not that she knew what they were crying about. Those guys were clearly not a big loss for the community. Nor were her other nine victims. Their idea of having fun was spending the night raping and torturing young girls.

She had not been very careful about the whole night, and when she thought about it, she wanted to hide, she was better than this. First, she forgot – or didn't want to – wear a wig, to at least hide her hair. Then, she spoke to some of the girls. SPOKE for fuck's sake. She had the strongest French accent that ever existed, and she had opened her damn mouth. And she went a bit crazy, adding ten more kills to her job, but how could she resist? Her other missions had been carried out with the discretion needed, but this last one was truly an epic failure, discretion wise.

She just wanted Senator Andrews, he was her target, the mayor was just a bystander. It wasn't 'til she was slicing his dick that she recognised him. Those bubble eyes, that thin mouth, and not a single hair on his scalp. But really it didn't matter, she didn't regret it one bit, she enjoyed it. There was no better feeling than the immense satisfaction she felt every time she spilled blood. And protecting women was her job, and they sure needed protection yesterday.

And kids...

Despite not being a mother, or intending to be one, Eve always had a thing for kids, and she damn sure hated paedophiles.

Sitting at her desk, she turned her computer on, wanting to check what women were saying on the Forum. Even if this was a "side hobby" to satisfy her bloodlust, she had to consider the opinions of her Guild, and their rules. Stupid rules, stupid rules which were meant to be broken. *Were they though?*

The screen lit up, and Eve went straight to the home page. It had been designed for women, with every taboo topic up for discussion. Here they could speak freely: rape, harassment, fear... whatever they needed. Some even organised face to face meetings.

World War III had endangered women, but it was especially hard for widows and orphans. While countries were mired in a despicable worldwide fight, women who stayed home had to deal with whatever cowards were left at the head of their countries. In many parts of the Western world those in charge tried to make their mark, creating numerous brothels and organising massacre games. When the war finally stopped, they ended the most gruesome activities, destroying the Reseau.

At least they were supposed to.

But unfortunately, a breach had opened, allowing the madness to return.

The soldiers like Eve had come home, tired and blood sick. She had stayed in France during the war, busy enough with a Civil War on top of the World War, and, like so many others, was so deep in the battle she didn't see the changes before it was too late.

And now here she was 5 years later feeling like it was 2035 again, dealing with the same issues that caused the damn war. The Suffragettes 2.0 movement had started in Canada as soon as the Armistice was signed, claiming, once again, what was due to women, and the Canadian government was now actively back in action, inciting the rest of the world to do the same.

It was as if the war was useless. All the extremist ideas they were fighting against were back, now replaced by the church.

She woke up post Armistice to a fully male-controlled country, limited work for women — even though they were the ones who kept the economy running during the war — abortion entirely forbidden in order to "fill the voids."

Those were some of the reasons why her Guild was created. The Forum was the official face of the organisation that came to her a few weeks after the Armistice, convincing her that her job was not done. Wracked with sleepless nights, stress, PTSD, and a thirst for what started as a job and a duty quickly became a hobby. Unlike most of her colleagues, it wasn't "just" for vigilante justice. She took a liking to killing during the war, and what better way than to take out her rage on assholes, right? She thought about visiting a counsellor a few times, but it was too late now, she was in too deep. The more she killed, the more she enjoyed it, the more she needed it.

There's no way out now.

Behind the girly façade of the website was a private message group, where her Guild allocated her missions. She could choose to accept or refuse the missions coming her way, but she really wasn't a "no" kind of girl. Killing bastards was just too much fun. And the Guild was at least directing her towards the right people to slaughter.

A soft 'meow' echoed from below, a warm, velvety touch following as something rubbed against her bare legs. She looked down, and smiled as a small, furry head bumped gently against her skin.

"Good evening my love," she murmured, stooping down to caress her new little black kitten. Neko purred with pleasure, immediately climbing on her lap. Neko nipping her fingers, Eve quickly glanced at a few topics, checking that everything was normal. She moved to check if there were any new registrants in her area, always taking the time to quickly investigate each of them, and closely monitored anyone who was too curious about the identity of the creators of the blog. She had yet to spot any false accounts. Women were working together even better than before, all allied against the new normal.

Sighing, she clicked on the icon to access her messages, hoping she wouldn't get in too much trouble for her failure. Her Guild leaders were not to be messed with. If anything went wrong, those women would be the first to betray her.

The purple interface appeared with a small envelope. She clicked on it, her stomach twisting in a way she would rather it not.

Good evening, Luna,

I saw the news on TV, CANADIAN TV FOR FUCK's sake. Nothing to be proud of, we will talk about it later. Try to play smart for a while.

"Trytoplaysmartforawhile," Eve grumbled, moving to look at the address and a name given to her.

Too late to cancel this one, just be smart and DISCREET

Her Guild Team Leader had gone as far as to write out the definition of the word "discretion," as if pulled from an actual dictionary.

"Bitch." Eve sighed. Smart and discreet were not always her forte.

Redirecting her attention to the television, she turned it back on to listen to what the 10pm news was saying about her. Thankfully there were no details about her features, yet, she was a little worried the girls she rescued would describe her.

Eve pouted, giving in to the realisation that her Guild Team Leader was right, she had been stupid. She would wear a wig next time, she normally ALWAYS did, but for some reason yesterday she decided it wasn't worth it. *Mistakes were made.*

She moved to the couch with Neko, who curled up on her lap, finally stopping his tiny bite attacks on her fingers. The news anchor, tremors in his voice and all, was still describing how cruelly the murderer had acted.

"Which cruelty?" she grumbled. "Bunch of fragile motherfuckers." Why were people giving her a bad time? *They should thank me for cleaning up.*

Her eyes narrowed on the men standing behind the news anchor. Three taller than average weird looking guys and what seemed to be Detective Mark, from Dublin Police, with his beige trench holding a coffee. *Cliché much?*

Eve frowned, her heartbeat stopping a split second before resuming its peaceful pace, but she straightened despite Neko's complaints. She wasn't an expert on gossip and stuff, but even she recognised Cyrus McRory and his two gorgeous right-hand friends, a redhead and a spiky blond. Their pictures were on the "TO BE WATCHED" wall at the police station.

Cyrus was heir to one of the biggest fortunes of Ireland, and a smart businessman. On the darker side of life, he was also known to be a fearsome gang leader and police enemy number one.

The giant....

Eve sat back on the couch, her mind ablaze. *What the hell is he doing there?*

According to some of her colleagues, Cyrus was certainly smarter and had much more resources than the police, he was rich, yes, and also had a reputation with the ladies, so she wondered if the brothel belonged to him. She remembered hearing gossips about him and his friends wiping out the infamous Reseau a few years ago, him in charge of a brothel didn't make any sense.

"He's way too hot to be a baddie... What do you think kitty?" Eve said, caressing Neko behind his cute little white ears. Kissing the fur ball, she put him down on the couch despite his plaintive meowing. Watching Cyrus on TV had triggered some memories she had tried to forget, another failure.

Shaking her head, Eve stood and went to her bedroom; she had some work to do and a GTL to make happy. And she had promised herself to bury the whole "almost died on a cruise ship" topic. Opening the door of her wardrobe, she stroked her "superhero" costume with her fingertips. The leather suit and gloves were a pitch black. Say whatever you wanted, but that was still the sexiest thing she could wear for her hobby.

Her mouth twisted, hesitation taking over. The address was only seven blocks away, she could easily walk there or run with a jogger's outfit. *It would be more discreet than Catwoman on a black motorcycle.* She pushed aside the sexy leather with a sad sigh, grabbing a sports tank top and her favourite black leggings before braiding her hair to bring it together in a crown.

Her hair was far too identifiable, and she knew she was being too confident, which according to all the Detective novels she had read was clearly one of the first mistakes serial killers made. She grabbed her small black backpack she used for her morning jogs and put her knife and gloves inside.

A shudder of excitement ran through her.

The blood is going to run again tonight.

DANGEROUS DOUBLE-JEU

23

Chapter 4

Cyrus

Cyrus, Ian, and Zorfield were in their favourite pub at the corner of Sandymon Green having a well-deserved Guinness, or eight. Per usual Ian and Zorf were out and about with the other patrons, singing, tap-dancing, and drinking while Cyrus was slouched in his favourite corner, staring blankly at the soon to be empty pint. His thick brow furrowed in a deep scowl, he couldn't get his mind to wander away from his day.

Not only had a brothel opened right under his nose with kids involved but knowing he was the prime suspect for two other horrific murders was truly nagging him.

Even Ian knew little about the crimes, but from what he gathered, this killer was busy kidnapping, torturing, and releasing the destroyed bodies of beautiful young women. Women who knew Cyrus. Around the 4th pint of Guiness Ian had started going into way too many details and theories about the murders, his profiler mind already in action but at Cyrus's look the redhead stopped.

As usual he was in the line of sight of all those idiots, especially freaking Cragnum. After all these years, the police and the media, not all, but many, continued to perceive him as the big bad wolf. He wasn't perfect for sure, but being considered a psychopathic rapist was a tad too much.

He grabbed his pint and gulped it down in one large sip, enjoying the roughness of the dark beverage on his tongue. Getting up to find his friends, he shook off his thoughts, wallowing was not his thing. He spotted Zorfield a bit further in the busy pub, standing on a massive wooden table perfectly executing his favourite tap-dancing choreography to the applauses and shouts of the drunks around him. Cyrus couldn't help but laugh at Ian, desperately trying to get Zorfield down. But quickly stopped when he saw the man sitting on the other side of the pub.

His ash-coloured hair and wearing his weird orange hunter fleece – Cyrus immediately recognized him, and too bad for him, Cyrus was going to enjoy beating the hell out of this guy right now.

He needed to release a bit of the tension in his shoulders, and the best way was either a sweet fight or a new woman to fuck, but the ones around tonight were all taken or ugly as fuck. *And if I fuck one and she dies tomorrow, I'll be in more trouble.*

Eve

The sound of her running shoes was far too noisy for Eve's liking. A little mix of blood and flesh not quite dried made it sound like she was crunching a snail. But one less abuser would be walking the streets tomorrow, a pretty big victory, compensating her ultimate failure last night. This kill was fast, efficient, and bloody. No witnesses.

A gust of wind reached her, making her shiver. Tightening her arms around her, she thought with regret about her unicorn hoodie back home.

Approaching the pub on her street, she started accelerating her pace while making less noise, an avoidance technique she had perfected over the years. And it wasn't that easy to do when you were coming back from a murder and your shoes had decided to squeak. The pub was always busy. Celtic music thumped through closed doors, always a bunch of drunkies on the sidewalk. Every time she passed, no matter if she was on the opposite side of the street or closer, she would hear whistles and catcalls addressed to her.

On the list of stuff she hated, this was at the top. The shame, the feeling of being barely just a dog you could whistle at. She had never liked it. It made her feel like a weak woman and Eve was NOT weak. But she couldn't kill all the men who did that, could she? *I mean...you could...*

Sometimes some of the men were brave enough to talk to her, standing in her way, only to be discarded like the piece of shit they were. But right now, she had no time to lose, there was no time for fun with the bloody butcher's knife and her trophy in her bag, both heavier than they should be on her shoulders.

At the absence of the usual calls, she couldn't stop her glance at the pub. *Did I managed to pass without being spotted?* That would be a first.

Oh.

The bar's patrons were too busy watching and sneering at a scene on the sidewalk. She had never seen them in that pub before.

Cyrus freaking McRory and his friends.

First on the TV, now here, on MY street.

A not so elegant "Oh shit" escaped her frozen mouth, a cloud of breath flying away. *This is bad for business.*

The one with the funny name she couldn't remember was lying on the hood of a big black car, his gaze seemed lost in the stars, while the other, with his long red hair braided behind his back, was leaning against the door, shaking his head in what appeared to be a gentle despair but not moving anyway.

And there he was, turning his back on his friends, his angry legs kicks stomping on a pile of rags.

The pile of rags was trying as much as he could to protect his face and his balls from the upset and quite inebriated Cyrus McRory. Eve wondered how many pints of Guinness it could take to get him drunk, only one was enough for her to feel like "weeeeeeeeeeeeee."

Under normal circumstance she would have jumped in to help the poor rag on the floor, and enjoy a quick fight, but she hesitated. The boys in this pub were always fighting at some point in the night. One of her favourite hobbies was to sit on her balcony with a glass of wine taking bets with herself on who was going to be the winner.

But Cyrus looked dangerous enough from a distance, and the stupidest thing to do right now would be to get his attention.

Lost in her thoughts she made the mistake of stopping, only realising it when the giant on the other side of the street locked her gaze. Eyes widened, she propelled herself at high speed, her sneakers squeaking.

"Re-shiiit," she mumbled. *Not goodnotgoodnotgood at all!*

"Cyrus! I can't believe you're dropping a fight for a chick!"

Did his friend sound outraged? She sure thought he did.

"You call this a fight?" Cyrus yelled, getting closer.

Having not yet decided to run as it would be perfectly ridiculous, she walked just a little faster to her street.

Catching up, Cyrus stood in front of her, his body blocking half the passage. *Note for later: update my priorities in life, and run!*

She sighed, giving the meanest look she could, going around the giant without letting go of her rude-girl look. *He should get the hint, shouldn't he?*

He grabbed her arm, pulling her towards him, his eyes looking down on her, a naughty smile on his lips.

Eve took a deep breath enjoying the view up close. Sure, he was scary, and obviously a "goujat" as she called them in her mothertongue, but her horny side focused on his full lips and the ocean eyes devouring her. His black t-shirt was almost perfectly moulded to his torso, and normally she would also have savoured his tight jeans revealing well drawn muscles, but her thoughts were swirling around the contents of her backpack. A knife was one thing, but the genital trophy, really? She had no idea what she would do with a bloody penis, she wasn't even sure her cat would want it for breakfast.

Another note for later: find out if cats are carnivorous enough to eat penises.

His wild bestial gaze upon her made her whole-body shudder. *Is it fear? Or are you just horny? Doesn't matter, I hate him.* He was tall, way too tall, far too manly and he looked at her as if he was going to eat her. Moving a tad closer, his hand had moved from her arm to her back, warm and steady, as he backed her against a car, moving her as if she was a doll.

Breathless, excitement took over, thinking how much fun it would be to have that stature and strength in her bed, with a hint of fear. She was not usually prone to fear, that detail not pleasing her.

Cyrus's smiled enlarged, one sexy as hell dimple appearing on his left cheek, and Eve was gone. As he got closer and closer, she knew her previous guesses were right, he was drunk.

She didn't dare move, uncertain of how to feel in this new dangerous and exciting bubble, her chest rising a little too high, a little too quickly for her liking. And when the man put both hands against the car, imprisoning her, his body so close to hers, she couldn't hold back a gasping noise. His face was so close she could feel his warm breath and couldn't help but shudder at that contact. He raised his hand, softly stroking her lips with his thumb and she knew he was going to be trouble.

"Cyrus... Do you really think we have time for that?" The redhead across the street sighed.

"Nah babe, let him have his fun." The blond laughed. "The day was tough."

The other sighed again. "Cyrus! We have enough trouble as it is."

The giant breathed a grunt of discontent, looked Eve in the eye while placing one of his arms behind her back again. He grabbed her face, dangerously bringing it to his until their lips met.

Oh.

It had been a long time since someone kissed her, especially in this way.

React! yelled her conservation instinct and feminist pride. The man bent in pain as his crotch met her knee.

She bolted out of the bubble, holding back a giggle. *That'll teach him to harass young innocent women alone on the street.* She sped up, reaching the entrance of her building, welcoming the safe feeling of the heavy door closing behind her.

Cyrus

Still in the street and carefully holding himself, Cyrus picked up an object, a smile on his lips. He returned thoughtfully to his friends, and without paying too much attention to Ian's disapproving gaze, he raised the pendant at eye level and frowned... he had seen this shark tooth somewhere...

He looked down the street where the girl disappeared, noting the building she had entered, searching his Guinness clouded memories trying to put a name to her pretty face.

"Cyrus, are you listening to me?" Ian asked, starting to get angry.

Cyrus looked at him with a disturbed look. "We know her, don't we?"

Chapter 5

Eve

Located in the heart of Dublin's city centre, the police building was a bustling hive, with officers mostly devoted to their daily tasks. On the ground floor sat the inspectors in the open space, some spending time playing cards, others looking at autopsy reports or statements, while others chatted around the room.

Eve let her eyes wander around the open space below her, sipping her coffee. She was at the end of the wooden staircase leading to the large glass window overlooking the waiting room of police Commander Erik Blondell. The building had seen better days, but Eve had rearranged her office with a feminine touch. That's right, her office.

The young woman almost did a cheery dance while gulping another bit of her bitter drink, she was glad nobody looked too much into her past, or else her extracurricular activities could become a problem for her day job.

Psychopath by night, devoted personal assistant to the police Commander by day. Damn you're good, girl.

Her and Erik met while she was in Australia just before the war, saving him and his wife during a storm in the open sea. They had gone their separate ways and after a few more years of travelling around the world, and her involvement during the war in France, Erik had contacted her again to propose a job so he could finish his position as the Commander surrounded by people he trusted, aka Miss Eve. She liked Erik, as far as men and bosses go, he was one of the good ones, and she knew he was taking his job seriously.

Eve almost jumped when she spotted Bonnie looking her way, and she waved quickly before retreating into her office, after all she didn't want the entire station to think she wasn't doing much all day while they were working their asses off.

Detectives Andy Murray and Bonnie Callen, The Dynamic Duo, were the top detectives in Dublin, and as far as Eve was concerned "good cops." She almost felt bad for them though, with all the murders going around - more than half of them her artwork - the Duo was doing whatever they could to keep the gruesome details of the women murders under wraps. She had heard them earlier complaining about the damn journalists, the biggest chain of television had started a contest to find the best nickname for the 11's killer. For now, Eve's favourite was "the Saviour." She thought it was a bit basic, but much better than "the Dick Slicer" like Andy had suggested.

One thing she wasn't happy about though was that her 11 kills of last weekend, almost overshadowed the two murders of young women that had taken place in recent weeks. Thankfully she could count on the Duo to stay focused, and even though they had been pulled into the 11's to give a hand to Mark, she could see the file on their desk of the young woman who had been found tortured and sliced last week.

Eve was not scared of Mark, he was fine as a Detective, but she didn't consider him a big enough threat. But Andy and Bonnie? She'd very much rather not have them on her back.

Busy working on the final details for Erik's travel, a seminar on criminology taking place in London, he was fond of human psychology, Eve was caught off guard when Cyrus Fucking McRory showed up in the door frame.

Shitshitshitshitshit she quite elegantly thought while blaming herself for her inner vulgarity, imagining the disapproving look her mother would give her if she was still around. The man stopped at the threshold, his gaze becoming more piercing, going through her again.

"If that's not luck...." he whispered, a smile on his lips.

"I wouldn't have put it that way." Eve boiled inside, wondering what he could be doing here. In her office. Hoping he didn't think it was weird for a young lady to go for a jog at 10:30pm.

While stress mounted with her thoughts going wild about how bad a jail outfit would look on her, Cyrus's friend appeared behind him. The redhead looked like he couldn't believe it either, his eyebrows so high they almost reached the top of his forehead. He gave Cyrus a little push so they could enter the office.

"Ian Rocfield." The redhead reached out to Eve with his hand, who looked at him with suspicion but appreciated the view. Long-haired, a soft blue-eye look and a lean figure, he was quite the opposite of Cyrus.

After a second of hesitation she held out her hand, remembering her good manners.

"Eve Vallon," she answered, shaking his hand. Her name had always been a mouthful to say, and it was worse when trying to have an English speaker understand her. She glanced at Cyrus still holding Ian's hand. "See? This is HOW you say hi to a young lady. Goujat".

Cyrus scoffed, she kind of hoped he didn't know the French word she loved to use.

"And this impolite man who shows up and thinks it's normal to harass young women on the street is Cyrus," Ian added, slipping an unequivocal glance at his friend.

Cyrus simply shrugged and walked towards Erik's door, not even looking at Eve. "I'll deal with you later, gorgeous."

His attitude got under Eve's skin, not only was he rude, but he also dared to disturb the Commander, her friend, in his office, without permission? This must be a crime for sure. *But he called you gorgeous.* She quickly stood up from behind her desk and rushed to block his path, her heels clicking on the wooden floor. Cyrus looked down at her from all his height with a smirk.

Cyrus

Ian sighed behind him.

"Do you have any idea who I am?" Cyrus asked, grabbing her chin, raising it so her eyes could only look at him. Two beautiful, hazel, angry eyes.

"No. And I don't give a flying fuck."

Cyrus, momentarily stunned, released his grip on her chin and she took the opportunity to give him a little slap on the wrist and slip away, making him rub his wrist in annoyance.

"This is the second time you've hit me. It better not become a habit."

"This is the second time you've ruined my day, so I guess we're even!" The little minx dared to smile at those words.

Cyrus burst out laughing and tried to grab her again, but this time she stood her ground. "Touch me and I will scream, loud! And I can guarantee that your detention will be very, very long!"

He was about to retort—

"Cyrus," Ian said firmly

"What?" Cyrus turned to him, exasperated.

"Sit. Now. I'm going home tonight and sleeping in my bed with my lovely blondie, and she's right, they won't let you through anyway, you saw the look Andy threw us when we arrived."

Cyrus looked at him and sighed, he hated Ian's habit of always being right. He went to sit while Eve returned to her desk, looking like she was trying to refrain from sticking her tongue out.

He was trying hard to remember where he knew her from, besides their street adventure. Ian remained silent, turning the pages of an architecture magazine he had picked from the table. Cyrus found it strange and looked at Ian who gave him an innocent look that clearly meant "I know who she is, but I won't tell you." Cyrus scoffed at his friend, and returned to watch the assistant's long legs, shameless.

Eve

Erik came out shortly after his appointment with Ser Lois Cragnum, a man notorious among the police, and whom Eve, for her part, found to be more than disgusting. But he was one of Ireland's powers, and above all, much to

Eve's displeasure, Erik's replacement when he would retire in a few weeks. She knew Lois had been known in the past for unglamorous facts, which he had miraculously managed to erase.

Even more, he persisted in meddling in police affairs, he was the one insisting the two recent women murders be looked at separately, refusing to allow the team to notify this as a serial killer.

Refraining an air of disgust, Eve thought about the two murders. Two women between 20 and 30 years old, one light-eyed beautiful blonde, typically Irish, the second, another kind of beauty, her long brown hair and darker eyes. According to the Duo, with the similar sadistic methods applied or close enough, there was no doubt the killer was the same person. You had to be blind or stupid not to conclude it was the work of a serial killer. Lois was not blind, despite his big black bushy eyebrows, so Eve concluded he was just stupid. And those women found tortured and dropped in the garbage like they were meaningless had her blood boiling.

Lois and Erik froze when they saw Cyrus, Lois displaying an expression of hatred and disgust, while Erik's had more an air of despair.

"Cyrus," Lois said, simply nodding.

"Asshole," Cyrus answered, not moving an inch.

Eve stifled a laugh, covering her mouth. Erik shot her one of his infamous disapproving looks, while Cyrus seemed rather proud, before she turned away, pretending to search through the closet behind her. Recovering she turned around as Lois scowled and bristled with discontent.

Cyrus stood, his threatening body towering over Lois, who just walked away, tail between his legs. Leaving Eve disgusted by his submission to the gang leader.

How did he ever make it to Commander?

Erik approached Cyrus. "You've got 10 minutes."

"I wanna talk about the murders."

Erik shook his head. "Which ones?"

Cyrus gave him a look that clearly meant "Do I look dumb to you?" his arms crossed over his chest; an eyebrow raised.

Erik sighed motioning them to his office.

Eve tried to listen as their voices grew louder, wondering if Cyrus was more interested in the psychopathic pervert killing young women, or her personal artwork? She sure wished it wasn't the latter, she didn't want to add the gang leader to her list of things to watch for. She heard Bonnie and Andy talking about his involvement in the investigation, and she was not happy about it.

The three men emerged from the office 10 minutes later, tension still high in the air. Erik ended the meeting whispering to Cyrus, trying to be discreet to avoid Eve's spied ears, but the young woman had a lot of practice at gossiping and hearing stuff she shouldn't.

"You know I can't take the risk Cyrus, not seven weeks away from my retirement for God's sake!"

"There will be more murders during those weeks," Cyrus sighed. "I have more resources than any police station in Ireland to search for this guy, but I need your information! Come on Erik!"

Relief washed over Eve, he was into the psychopath killer, and she couldn't stop a little cheerleader dance, wriggling on her chair.

Cyrus paused, walking towards Eve, glancing at her legs before slowly turning away. "Not to mention, why do you have different teams on it? It's obvious that's the start of a serial killer, even I know that without having all the details, and I'm not that smart."

Erik sighed, exchanging a look with Eve, both very well aware Lois was the reason why.

"These murders don't concern you Cyrus, please." Erik shook his head. "A lot of things will change with me leaving, and you should prepare to back off now."

Cyrus smirked. "Do you think that fat pig scares me? He trembles like a woman in front of me."

Eve pouted, that was not fair for women.

"And besides. I lied, I know very well why you people are not working that hard on it." Cyrus gave a pressed look at Erik, who pulled his shoulders back, glancing at Cyrus and Ian.

"I'm not sure what you heard Cyrus, better not believe all the gossips running wild in the station, you know better."

The giant sniggered, shaking his head, Eve was not that sure what they were talking about, maybe she needed to improve her spy-skills.

"When he's in power, things will be different. And one of his first goals will be to bring you down, believe me, he's not being silent about it." Erik stood tall, trying to sound firm. "You have other things to focus on. Let us take charge of the murders. DON'T get involved in the investigation. Neither this one nor the case of the Saviour. "

Eve nodded in agreement, but Cyrus shook his head, clearly unconvinced. "We'll see."

Erik quickly walked towards Eve, who was holding his travel documents and briefcase, and she gave him an encouraging smile. She really appreciated Erik, he and his wife were two of the most adorable people she'd ever met. "Ok Cyrus I have to go...."

Cyrus remained still.

"...Maybe I'll take you to the door?"

"No thank you, I have to take care of something with your adorable assistant first."

"I...."

"It's okay Erik, you're going to miss the plane, I'll take care of it." Eve smiled.

Her fears from the other night seemed to have vanished as she suddenly remembered her own ability to defend herself against perverts. Now, the only thing was to manage her own behaviour so she could convince Cyrus she was just a cute little fragile woman.

Erik didn't seem very happy but checking the clock on the wall, he hastened his way towards the exit, throwing a last glance towards Eve before leaving.

Eve turned to Cyrus giving the meanest and firmest look possible. But it didn't seem to impact the giant that much, as he advanced towards her with his annoying sneer. Ian let out a louder than necessary sigh of exasperation, but it didn't stop his friend. The giant placed his enormous hands on Eve's desk, and she raised an eyebrow that was both questioning and disdainful. Still no reaction from the giant.

"Do you need something maybe?" she asked.

"Dinner with you would be the perfect way to end this wonderful day," Cyrus replied, serious.

Seriously?

Ian didn't seem to believe it either, given his expression. "Ok Cyrus, I don't want to see your demise, I'm waiting for you outside!!" he laughed.

Cyrus turned towards his friend, scoffing. "I'm glad to see my best friend doesn't believe in my power of seduction!"

"He's right!" Eve started packing her belongings, hoping it would make it clear that she was leaving as well. "I'd rather go and eat with Lois than with you. At least he doesn't assault poor, single, perfectly innocent women in the street!" *Okay girlfriend, slow down.* That was a lie, Lois was disgusting, and she would rather fuck Cyrus 100 times over than give 10 seconds of her time to Lois, but still.

"Oh sweetie! I'm not the one here who hit the other," Cyrus added with a half-dark, half-laughing look.

"You started it!" Eve replied, outraged.

Cyrus scoffed. "Indeed. I find it hard to resist legs like those, not to mention that irresistible little French accent you're trying to hide." He paused his look darkening. "And believe me, you really don't want to be alone with your soon to be boss."

What did he mean? Sure Lois didn't have what could be called an excellent reputation, but it was mostly a cowardly one, though perhaps there was something even darker underneath it all. Which could become quite exciting for her if he turned out to be a rapist or something. Or maybe Cyrus was playing with her, she'd always tended to be too gullible. She sighed.

"All of this to say, no, I'm not going out with you. Not to mention that given YOUR reputation, it would be very bad if I show up in broad daylight on the arm of the big villain McRory." She rose from her seat intending to gently but firmly redirect Cyrus towards the exit. But he grabbed her hips, drawing her closer to him.

How big are those hands?

Eve bite her lip, thinking about all the nice things they could do to her body.

"Soooo... you do know who I am," he said with a victorious smile, making Eve's eyes widen in front of her own stupidity. She felt so small and fragile, her body moulded perfectly against his mighty body.

They exchanged a glance for a few seconds, his eyes were not black as she had first believed, but more of a deep blue, like a shade of an angry ocean. They seemed to penetrate her, reading deep within her. Cyrus's hand slipping along her back pulled her out of her stupor, and she tried to free herself. Which wasn't easy.

"Cyrus," she murmured, looking him straight in the eye. "Let go of me."

He merely smiled lowering his hand until he reached her buttocks. Shuddering, she tried to free herself in a more convincing manner, but Cyrus caught her firmly under both buttocks. She let out a little scream, as he lifted her, placing her on her desk. The situation was completely out of control, here she was, sitting on her own desk at the police station, being manhandled by one of Ireland's most feared men!

Wake up girlfriend! ...Or maybe just close the office blinds and pull down his pants...

Her mind began to stray, imagining the wild love they could make on her desk, especially if his dick was proportional to his hands. But when she saw what Cyrus held in his hand, her favourite pendant, she looked at him angrily.

"How did you find this? It's mine! Give it back to me!!" Snarling, she tried to grab the necklace while pushing Cyrus away with her other hand; but it seemed to have no effect on the giant in front of her.

"Cyrus!!" Ian had his hands on his hips seeming furious, standing in the doorway. "Can I ask what you think you're doing ???"

"I'm negotiating!" Cyrus replied with a smile, continuing to escape Eve's swiping, which seemed to have no effect on him.

"Give it back to me Cyrus! "

"Cyrus for God's sake, just behave yourself!" Ian sighed.

"Tonight at 8:00?" Cyrus turned to Eve.

"You're dreaming!"

"Cyrus, don't force me to intervene," Ian threatened.

"Oh please!!" Cyrus laughed.

"My necklace!!"

"8pm tonight." Cyrus grabbed Eve's wrists, pulling them ferociously behind her back. "8pm and I give you back your necklace at the end of the meal in exchange for nothing else."

She let her breath calm a little, tried to free herself without much conviction, and finally nodded, making a sulky face.

Fiiiine, I'll go on a date with this sexy man of Neandertal.

"Perfect."

"You don't have my address." Eve pouted.

"Oh don't worry, I already have everything I need."

Eve looked at him uncertain, where had he been able to find her address? She had only just moved in, and she couldn't help but wonder what else he knew? She hoped he was only referring to silly stuff like her phone number and last name, and not her extracurricular activities.

Cyrus left the room with his eternal smile, joining an exasperated Ian, who glanced a sorry look at Eve before following his friend outside.

Eve shook her head, trying to regain her composure, this man sure knew how to turn her on. This was bad, this was SO bad. She couldn't decide if she hated him, admired him, or wanted him... all options being unreasonable. But he had her pendant hostage, and she wasn't going to let it go without a fight.

She picked up her belongings, put on her green raincoat — she had thought wearing a green raincoat would make of her a real Irishwoman but she had forgotten that real Irish women never wear jackets, no matter the weather — and descended the stairs leading to the ground floor, where a few of her colleagues were still working, despite the incoming weekend. Eve quickly passed by Johnny Jefferson, nodding with a clenched smile, the minimum effort she could do while still looking natural. He always looked at her with a disgusting libido driven look. *That guy's a pig.* She didn't know where she drew this information from, she just knew it. Her killer instinct had to be useful sometimes.

Taller than average, a prominent belly due to the abuse of beer and the non-abuse of sport, a globular look, luscious lips like those of a woman and a colour far too pink for a man of this age. Jefferson reminded her of the groupers she had previously encountered during her many diving expeditions.

She stopped a little further away to chat with the Duo, greeting Andy and Bonnie, whom she particularly appreciated. They were quite the explosive duet, physically and personality wise. Andy was as blond as Bonnie was brown thanks to Mexican origins. Only her skin colour and her singing accent reminded you of it though. Andy stood at almost 1m90 while she was a mere 1m60, leading some of their colleagues to mock her at first - until she took them down in five seconds flat.

Andy had what people called a bad character, he liked to complain, and he didn't hide his thoughts about other cops or politicians. The only person he would confide in without hesitation was his partner. Though he seemed to enjoy Eve's company as well, and right now both seemed to be relieved to find a reason to look away from their file, where Eve caught a quick glimpse at the photos filled with blood.

A shudder took her, maybe she should take care of it herself... but investigating was really not her forte. Give her a name, an address, and a reason and they could talk.

"Hi sweetie," said Bonnie with a smile, then she sighed closing the file.

"Your turn." She threw the thin file on Andy's desk, and without paying attention to the man's grumbling she grabbed another one.

"Which one is this?" Eve asked, her head slightly tilted to read the information.

"That's the Dick Slasher!"

Bonnie gave big eyes to Andy, while nodding imperceptibly towards Eve.

"Sorry," Andy muttered, who didn't seem that sorry.

"You mean the 11's? That's such a crazy story." The good side of being a pretty little thing with a cute accent was that it was always quite easy to play dumb. And Andy fell right into her trap.

"That's a fucking complicated one, those witnesses are all crazier than the others, and now freaking Cyrus McRory is looking into it."

Bonnie sighed, interrupting her grumpy partner, whispering to Eve. "Mark told us as soon as he came back the other day that Cyrus was probably going to get involved... This boy can't stop himself from meddling in police business."

She stopped and looked at Andy. "That's why this one here has been a pain in my neck all day, thinking I can't hear him grumbling."

Eve chuckled while Andy rolled his eyes.

"You're grumbling too, you think I don't hear you swearing in Spanish all fucking day long?"

"I'm grumbling because as usual, perverse politicians are more important to the public than unknown young women tortured and raped to death."

Eve bit her lip, having the decency to feel bad for one second, she had not planned her killings to shadow the others.

"There's also this new one," Andy continued, "missing a dick too. I'm telling you, those are linked. Bonnie found out this morning that the man was known for his ambiguous role during the war, but more importantly he was a friend of at least half of the brothel customers."

"Well," Bonnie interrupted, "we can't be certain that's the same killer"

"Either that or someone out there thinks slicing dicks off is a great idea." Andy sniggered avoiding the pen Bonnie threw his way, then came back to his serious self turning to Eve. "What did McRory want from the chief?" He was staring sharply at her, as if he were ready to use any answer to jump straight on Cyrus and finally handcuff him. Everyone at the station knew it was one of his dearest wishes.

Eve smiled faintly. "Nothing special I think... And why does this man have that much power in this country? In Dublin? And in the police station?" she asked gesturing towards the room. Her "what-the-fuck" face was on, eyes wide open and one eyebrow raised, but she didn't care.

Andy sighed, exchanged a quick glance with Bonnie who shrugged, then looked at Eve with an inquisitive and mysterious air, as if to question if she deserved to be put in the confidence of the greats of this world.

"Because he has everything that can lead a world: money, power, and fear," Andy explained. "He paid for some of the equipment in the precinct you know, like the gym, the swimming pool... brand-new computers... pay-checks..."

Eve's eyes widened, she knew there was some money story hiding, but a mafioso paying for the police equipment? That was almost sad to hear. No wonder he held power over Erik and Cragnum. *Money! Money! Money!*

"I heard he is the richest man in this damn country," Andy said, twirling a pen between his fingers. "and the worst part about it is that most of his money is not even illegal now," he added with regret in his voice.

Eve wasn't sure she would qualify this as the worst thing ever, but what did she know?

"And, even worse, a large part of the people here would give their lives for him. He knows how to put the poor in his pocket. He was a war hero, and people remember that. " Andy leaned back into his seat "Don't worry about it darling, stay away from him, he likes pretty women," he added, stirring his pen in her direction. "And two of those pretty women are dead now."

Cold invaded Eve's chest, now that was a detail she was not aware of. *Did I just agreed to go on a date with a freaking psychopath?*

"Andy!" The look Bonnie sent her partner was that of a mother reprimanding her toddler. Andy shrugged his shoulders snickering as Bonnie turned back to Eve, her heart about to beat out of her chest.

"He is not the monster they say he is. And ANYONE with a bit of common sense—" she glanced at Andy who had the good measure to look at the file in front of him "—would know that Cyrus probably has nothing to do with those horrific murders." She sighed. "Yes, Cyrus is certainly not a very recommendable boy, BUT," she looked down at her colleague "he is one of the very few people of high influence in this city, whom you CAN trust."

She turned back to Eve's astonished eyes. "No conspiracy, no political bribes, no human trafficking. Maybe a few police bribes here and there," she added with a smile while Andy barked, still eyeing his files. "And I think all the cops appreciate the subsidies coming from Cyrus McRory. He also does have better behaviour than many drug dealers OR politicians. Do you know why we're nervous about him meddling in the investigations?"

Eve shook her head, not wanting to interrupt Bonnie while she was on a roll. She was fascinated by her sublime accent, already seeing herself on dream beaches sipping a Pina Colada.

"The neighbourhood where we found the girls, and also the 11's but that's a different killer..." — *You bet it is.* — "that's HIS neighbourhood. If you go there and you cause trouble, you may not last long."

"I live there," Eve mumbled.

"Do you cause trouble?" Andy asked, raising his head from the file he was fake reading.

"Of course not." We*ll, you know, a murder here and there.*

Bonnie waved her hand, bringing back Eve's attention to her. "He's bound to get involved in everything that happens, even if Erik said no." She paused, showing a funny face, exchanging a look with Andy. "And that, on the other hand, will certainly not be done in a very legal way. Cyrus is very good at making people disappear. And no one can resist Cyrus McRory." She blushed a bit but came back to her serious self quickly, giving a suspicious look to Eve, who felt the heavy gaze coming from Andy as well. "Well, it's still better not to hang out with him anyway. He might not be a bad guy, but he is for sure a bad boy."

Eve no longer knew where to hide, could they read her face and the mixed feelings she had for this man? She always had a thing for bad boys. She hoped her tan would somewhat hide the redness she felt creeping on her cheeks, so she simply nodded, holding back "yes mommy." They exchanged a few more words, and then she finally left.

She had a date to prepare for, and a reputation as a femme fatal French woman to uphold.

And I do love bad boys.

45

Chapter 6

Eve

After running the last metres under a cool rain which took her by surprise, *Welcome to Ireland!* Eve finally climbed the steps leading to her floor. Relief flooding her as she opened the door of her small apartment. She had been lucky to find this small slice of heaven in the perfect neighbourhood. Cyrus's neighbourhood.

Well, lucky and helped by Erik, considering this was one of his investments propriety. The flat was basic but perfect, the door opened on a short corridor ending in the open kitchen. The kitchen was tiny but given her limited cooking skills it worked. The most important for her was the master bedroom.

She left her shoes in the first few metres of the entrance, throwing them away from her poor feet, hoping to avoid wearing torturous heels until Monday. She walked to her bathroom so she could try to look like a captivating woman for the evening.

After all, she had a plan. Get to know Cyrus to keep a close watch on him. In her mind there was no way this could go wrong.

After lathering in the warm shower, she went to inspect her potential outfits, it had been a long time since she had dressed for someone other than herself. Her gaze wandered for a few seconds on her photo wall, which she had fun creating during one of the many rainy afternoons. It was mostly pictures of her time in Oceania. Memories flooded back of the countless hours spent on her boat, exploring the Islands, the warm reception from the Aboriginal people. The dives with Bruce.

The precious necklace she wanted back so badly was all she had left from him... one of his teeth. The great white shark seemed to enjoy turning around Eve during her dives. Terrified at first, she screamed in her mouthpiece, already imagining the gruesome death coming to her, a death that never happened. The shark just chilled.

Sometimes it seemed she had lived three lives, perfectly distinct. The Pre-War, the War, and the Post-War. She shook her head, refocusing her mind on the present, deciding to divert her attention back to her outfits.

"So..." she began, addressing her reflection in the mirror. "Little red dress? Or little black dress?" She alternated between the two outfits in front of the full-length mirror, observing her image. Years spent outside and her dedication to fitness had sculpted Eve's body, of which she was now quite proud of. Her long and slender legs had always been a prominent feature, and the red dress was undeniably sexy, accentuating her figure with its form-fitting material that left little to the imagination. Its deep V-neckline was one of the daring variety and she could already imagine Cyrus's eyes being diverted. She swapped quickly for the black dress, while slightly less eye-catching, it exuded its own allure, boasting a modest length with a captivating open back that would reveal her tanned skin.

Eve let out a frustrated sigh. Why bother trying to look beautiful for this scoundrel? She tossed the dresses on the floor and picked up her favourite pair of jeans, the ones with holes in the knees. She paired them with a green top to complete the outfit, along with her trustworthy green sneakers. Looking at herself in the mirror she felt rather satisfied. At 29, she easily appeared at least 5 years younger.

She was about to go brush her bushy hair when a knock on the door stopped her, she didn't think he would be early! Eve looked up, puzzled, someone could have opened the door of the building but how did he know her floor? And what about her apartment number? She released her hair, and it cascaded down her back, wild brown curls bouncing in all directions. Annoyed, she headed to her front door opening it, attempting to maintain a cold and impassive expression in the presence of the giant standing before her.

His gaze quietly lingered on her figure, burning with intensity, fixating on her unruly hair. She moved away from the door and the imposing man simultaneously, ensuring he had no opportunity to let his hands wander. Cyrus entered the apartment surveying the small space. He shrugged an inquisitive eyebrow before turning to Eve who promptly closed the door.

"You're early, I'm not ready."

"I can see that, go get changed, we are gonna be late."

"Oh no, my outfit is fine, I'm talking about my hair." She pointed to her sparse mass of hair, not resisting giving Cyrus a childish but always efficient "duh!"

Cyrus scoffed, leaning against her kitchen island, arms crossed on his way-too-large-and-manly torso, making Eve look a bit too close at how the shirt was pulling on his full arms.

"The place we are going to, my beautiful Eve, is quite classy and I don't want to be seen with an ordinary young woman, especially when you are worth much more than that."

Eve pouted but continued to defy him, not moving an inch towards her closet.

"Well I'm not changing, I am afraid we might need to cancel our date then". *Don't stick your tongue out at him, don't stick your tongue out at him, you are a grown ass lady.*

"Genevieve."

Eve had a moment of stupor, how in the living hell did he know her name? *Genevieve.* What were her parents thinking when they named her? She had been using Eve as a nickname for as long as she could remember.

"Saying my full name is not gonna work on me Cyrus." But it worked. It totally worked.

She could feel her heartbeat faster as a familiar sensation between her legs ignited a long-forgotten fire. The giant moved away from the kitchen island slowly, advancing towards her. His right hand flew over to one of her crazy bouncy curls, twirling it, pensively. Their eyes met, hers defiant, his playful.

"I never take no for an answer, my Goddess."

Eve scoffed, and before she could answer something smart, he pulled her towards his strong body, a hand firm on her lower back, whispering in her ear.

"I have the power to make you do better. Willingly, or forcibly. And in case you didn't know yet, the thought of being able to undress you so early in the evening before I buy you dinner is really enticing."

Eve shuddered, tension hanging in the air, her thoughts racing as she debated whether to retreat to her room immediately and change to avoid any potential trouble. She could perfectly imagine him ripping her clothes off, hopefully he would let her rip his off as well. But this was going way too fast.

"Fine, whatever." She pushed him back to get away and felt his heavy look on her until she closed her bedroom door. Taking a deep breath, she decided on the slutty black dress, and a few minutes later opened the door as violently as she could, expressing her discontent, which barely made Cyrus smirk.

He let his eyes roam her figure, up and down. "Perfect. Don't touch your hair," he added as she started to put her hair in a bun. "I like a bit of wildness in my life"

The comment made her eyes roll as she headed towards her shoe closet. Glancing in regret at her green sneakers, she grabbed a pair of black and gold heels, they would make the back of the dress sexier. *Looking for trouble again la la la la.*

She put on her shoes, but even with them on, she still felt so tiny compared to Cyrus, who was gazing at her with his calm but burning eyes. She would not be surprised if he reached 2m height, the guy was a freaking giant. They left the apartment building, and Eve reluctantly accepted Cyrus's offered arm while rolling her eyes again, which made Cyrus chuckle slightly.

He escorted her to his car, an enormous black 4x4 - *so typical!* - and even opened the door for her. She wasn't quite sure what to make of this gallantry. Her feminist side found it rather ridiculous, while a buried, romantic, girly side within her found it thrilling. She appreciated the cleanliness of the car, which she didn't expect, and tried to relax. Expecting more of a cliché, she thought she would have to push aside beer cans and maybe cigarette packets. Even some used condoms, nothing would surprise her.

She felt Cyrus's presence in the car and turned to him with a questioning look. Cyrus simply maintained eye contact and started the car, which only fuelled Eve's inner frustration.

The ride went in silence, Eve fidgeting in her seat, while Cyrus drove smoothly, respecting all speed limits and stopping at every pedestrian crossing. She couldn't help but wonder whether he did it out of genuine respect for traffic rules, or, as her preferred explanation, to annoy her even more.

After what felt like an eternity, they finally reached their destination. Even though she had nothing to complain about - *I mean, besides the fact he threatened to rip off your clothes earlier* - her perpetual state of indecision was not making things any easier.

On one hand, she believed getting to know Cyrus would not only protect her activities but also potentially aid in identifying the psycho killer.

On the other hand, she simply wished to get rid of him to avoid putting her second life in unnecessary danger. Not to mention the temptation. He did have a fine butt after all.

She stepped out of the car without waiting for him to open the door, giving him a mini provocative glance as she passed by, which once again elicited an enigmatic smile from him. *God he is so annoying!* Looking around, she recognised the rather chic neighbourhood of Ballsbridge which had been spared during the war. Boasting several intact wealthy mansions, designer shops she would certainly never set foot in, despite all the money she owned, and some of the best restaurants in Dublin. She wondered if Cyrus intended to display his wealth thinking it would impress her, she wasn't particularly passionate about money or the way men related to it. However, her love for food might be her downfall.

They made their way towards a massive building made entirely of glass, The Fall, the tallest building in Ireland, home to some of the major corporations. Holding an excellent Japanese restaurant on the top floor she had heard a lot about. She couldn't help but feel a hint of excitement, her stomach fluttering, she loved Japanese cuisine and their customs. They entered the building, and while a few dozen people patiently waited in line for the security check, Cyrus slipped through, if one could use the verb for a man of this stature, and simply nodded at one of the three guards, who stood up at once and stepped aside to let them pass.

Eve took a deep breath when the room gazed upon them, whispers ensuing. If she was lucky, they would assume she was just another silly and rather cute conquest. She silently prayed no paparazzi were around, the thought of her explaining to Erik why her picture was on the first page of the Dublin Glamour was not as exciting as it sounded.

As they entered the lift and watched the door close, Cyrus turned to her, approaching dangerously close. Eve stiffened, pressing herself against the partition, once again stopping him by placing her index finger against his chest. Cyrus halted and simply stared into her eyes, causing Eve to swallow, hating herself.

"You're not very talkative tonight, my beautiful Frenchy," he whispered, drawing his face closer to hers.

"The deal was not for me to talk." She stuck out her tongue.

Cyrus burst out laughing "Stop acting like a kid, I'm sure you'll love this restaurant. And if you're not gonna use this tongue of yours for something good, you should keep it in." One of his naughty smiles lit his face, his eyes burning the very little will Eve had.

"I won't even bother to answer that last comment. ANYWAY, I am sure the restaurant is amazing, too bad we had to book at least three weeks in advance to get a table."

"When you own the place, a simple phone call is enough," Cyrus replied with a big smile, showcasing his sparkling teeth.

"When... what?? You own the restaurant?" Eve exclaimed, astounded. "I've never heard that the great McRory was interested in culinary art!"

"People talk a lot but don't know anything about me." He uttered the last words as he leaned closer to Eve's face, his warm breath reaching her neck. Eve froze, a finger still in the air mumbling something incomprehensible. The doors opened and she turned, heading towards the restaurant, fully aware Cyrus was not only sneering at her back but also watching her backside.

She couldn't help but accentuate the movement of her hips, knowing the power of a feline gait over men, while sweeping her mass of hair to the right side of her face to free the view. She tapped her fingers inwardly for playing with fire, but she had always had this seductive side.

Cyrus caught up with her, and as they advanced side by side towards the restaurant reception, he slid his hand between the thin fabric of the dress and her back. A shiver ran through her body, goosebumps covering her arms. Cyrus had just enough time to whisper "pretty dress" before giving his attention to the young Japanese beauty at the entrance and spoke, much to Eve's surprise, in Japanese.

She looked at Cyrus puzzled, she had no idea he was capable of speaking this language, and moreover to perfection, herself being close to fluent in the magnificent language. She had to admit, if she put aside Cyrus's overly touchy-dominating-do-what-I-say side, he was quite surprising compared to what she had heard about him.

Even his appearance impressed her, the man was elegant, not too much nor too little. He had chosen a fairly classic pair of black trousers that accentuated his legs and muscular buttocks... something she shouldn't even have noticed. And a nice white shirt helped show off his body more than nicely. Though, he still lacked refinement in the context of the upscale restaurant, with the last button of his shirt undone, revealing a torso covered in what seemed to be a fair amount of hair. So manly. Not to mention his long hair, which he hadn't bothered to tie up. *Does he tie it up during sex?* Eve rolled her eyes at her own thought, she definitely needed to stop thinking about him sexually.

But she continued counting on her fingers the months since she had some kind of sex abruptly stopping when she felt Cyrus and the young Japanese waitress staring at her.

"Are you ready to go to our table or are you still looking for an escape route?" Cyrus asked mockingly.

"Second solution," Eve replied, before following a young woman wearing a stunning blue and white outfit, blending the elegance of the kimono with a practical outfit required for working in a restaurant. The waitress led them, and Eve, who had become a master at Evelyzing people's reactions, guessed a certain surprise in her. Seeing the great McRory with a woman, which, let's face it, was not only amazing but flattering to Eve.

As they made their way to their secluded table, which unfortunately seemed to be at the farthest end of the restaurant and far too private, much to Eve's dismay, Cyrus acknowledged the other guests with nods here and there but did not stop for anyone. Eve could feel their looks upon her, them and hated it. *So much for discretion.*

Eve surprised herself by praying to an unknown god that no one in the police would find out.

They finally reached their table, which was indeed at the very end of the restaurant, in a corner, hidden to everyone's eyes. The table was half-moon-shaped, leaning against a glass wall offering an incredible view of Dublin's illuminated skyline, a view that delighted Eve. However, her delight was short-lived when the young Japanese woman deftly closed the curtains, ensuring complete privacy for the couple.

Oooh not good, not good at all.

Of course, Cyrus used the opportunity to get closer, only to be stopped in his tracks as she placed her finger on his chest, AGAIN, raising an eyebrow, AGAIN.

"I prefer to keep my distance."

Cyrus laughed. "That may be difficult given the outfit you're wearing tonight. You're gorgeous."

The compliment made Eve uncomfortable, and she tried to regain some composure by grabbing a menu, attempting to hide her blushing cheeks. The curtains opened revealing Akito, Eve finally saw her badge, who elegantly placed a bottle of red wine on the table, first showing the label to Cyrus, who gave a small wave of the hand before serving Eve a drink.

Clearing her throat, trying to forget about the close presence of the giant, she found the courage to ask her burning question. "How did you come to own a Japanese restaurant?"

He took his time to respond, turning his glass between his fingers, taking a moment to savour its aroma.

"I like investing, I do have some *legitimate* business ventures." He winked. "I tasted the chef's kitchen in Tokyo three years ago, and managed to lure him away and convince him, and his family, to come here and open one of the finest restaurants this city has ever known." He took a sip of his wine. "We were nearing the end of the war, and I knew I had to protect my pretty ass when I got home. When you have a bad reputation, some people tend to forget what you did to save their skin," he added bitterly. "And the Irish love what's exotic. Akito is one of his daughters, she will inherit the restaurant at some point, but if she wants to open a business here I am committed to providing her with the necessary funds. To her and her three brothers and sisters."

Eve was quite impressed but tried not to show it, securing financing for a business had become a luxury after the war, and only a few fortunate could take the risk of starting anew.

Eve made a mental note to investigate why the police and politicians hated the man, besides the mafioso thing, obviously. She didn't know the whole history of Ireland during the war, perhaps she should also inquire about the actions of the Golden Boy. Given what she had heard about the gentleman's character it was more than possible he had shed his share of blood as well. It was war and given her own actions in France she was in no position to blame him for a few murders.

Akito returned to take their order, and Eve became agitated, having not had time to read the fabulous menu.

"Do you want to share a boat of all the chef's specialties?" Cyrus asked.

"Yes, perfect." Eve handed her menu to Akito and as the young woman left, Cyrus turned a bit more towards Eve, resting his arm on her chair, smiling when Eve stiffened a little.

"Are you always on your guard like that? Or just with me?"

"Always." Eve smiled.

"Well, there are many freaks around us to be fair," he said before taking a sip of wine.

"No kidding, I'm at the restaurant with one of them right now."

Cyrus almost choked on his wine but eventually started laughing.

"My goodness Eve, you are one of the few people I've met in my life who isn't even a tiny bit afraid of me," he said with a serious air.

Eve praised herself for her ability to hide her feelings, truth was she hadn't been so frightened by anyone for a long time.

"At your service," she said raising her glass for a toast.

"I'm serious," Cyrus continued, "the only people who aren't frightened by my presence are my two best friends, Ian and Zorfield, and possibly my mother. Everyone else shudders when I speak, pushes each other out of the way when I walk in."

"On the other hand, I will not blame anyone for not wanting to be crushed by this…" Eve pointed to his body with her head, which again triggered a laugh in the giant.

To her surprise the conversation continued quite pleasantly, with some restraint on her side, and carefully chosen topics by Cyrus. Like, how did she get to work with the Irish police, specifically to assist a Commander so close to retirement? Eve relaxed a little, she was always wary of people asking too many questions, but Cyrus seemed open, and unlike many others he didn't hide his inquiries behind a veil of hypocrisy. He simply asked the question.

Despite this, she found herself a little embarrassed and shy, it had been a long time since anyone had asked details on her life to which she intended to answer, and not just add lie after lie. So she had to be careful what she said or didn't say. As for her relationship with Erik that was the easiest part.

"I had a small travel company in Australia, I took tourists on sailing tours to the most famous corners of the country. One day, I was by myself away from the tourist spots to dive with the sharks. But very quickly I saw another boat seeming to sail freely and a storm was about to break out."

Eve smiled as she recalled that day, when Erick and his wife had come face to face with Bruce in the water. She would have sworn she heard their screams suffocate in their masks.

"Erik and his wife were in trouble in the water. I took them back to their boat. End of story. Don't tell him I told you though." She paused a fraction of a second. "Actually, don't tell him anything, AT ALL."

"Hmmmmm." Cyrus's eyes widened. "Did you just say… Sharks?"

"Ahem… Yes. They're not as dangerous as we think."

Cyrus seemed to consider the question for two seconds only to finally burst out laughing. "I would love to swim with sharks! And would have paid dearly to see Erik's head when he first came across her." He took a deep breath. "I've always wanted a private aquarium I could throw my enemies in."

Eve almost choked on her wine as a snarky smile played on his lips. She placed a hand on her mouth, holding back a laugh, but the giant continued the conversation as if nothing happened.

"I'm guessing that explains the funny necklace pendant you were wearing. So you and Eric are... friends?"

"Um yes, I guess we can say that. We weren't in contact during the war, I guess we were too busy on our own. After the war I went to Canada — *you are saying too much girl, stop right now!* — and after a while I wanted to come back to Europe. And I've always loved Ireland. Erik needed someone... to trust... I don't think I'm teaching you anything about current politics?"

Cyrus scoffed. "Not at all. Finding trusted employees has become difficult. Many people have tried to survive the hard way, and some bad habits from the war have remained."

Eve wasn't sure what he meant by that.

"We lost the extremist invaders and ended up with extremists in our own country. I am not surprised you went to Canada, it was one of the only countries where women didn't lose their full rights."

A feminist bad boy. This was amazing. Eve didn't know how to react. She definitely had to stay on her guard.

"Indeed," she said cautiously, "and those men jumping on you in the street out of nowhere are THE WORST."

Cyrus laughed again then bent down over her, gazing with his dark look, Eve gulped, her heart racing again, the desire to feel his hand on her skin coming out of nowhere.

"I didn't say I was perfect, as my behaviour with you will attest. You are temptation." He brushed a soft finger along Eve's jawline, down her neckline, and to her displeasure, he stopped right at the edge of the fabric.

Eve sighed, and without a word, caught the giant's hand placing it where it belonged, on her breast.

His body tensed, holding back one of his sarcastic smiles, but he kept his hand on the curve. She crossed her legs, trying to stop the fire in her loins, but she didn't let go of Cyrus's eyes, which were getting heavier and full of desire by the second. She moaned when his fingers pinched her sensitive nipple through the fabric, pulling, turning, rubbing it between his expert fingers. Laying her head back on the giant arm behind her, she internally cursed herself for openly flirting with Cyrus. *THIS.WAS.NOT.THE.PLAN.*

This said, she whined when Cyrus let go of her breast and sat back in his chair, pulling lightly on his pants, trying to get comfortable.

Akito arrived with their order — *he must have seen her somehow* — Eve still in shock and feeling her entire body blushing, tried to sit straight awing at the huge wooden boat filled with delicious Japanese food.

The only kind of sex I'm having tonight is the starfish-kind.

Chapter 7

Eve

As promised, it was with a full and content belly that Eve and Cyrus finally left the restaurant. She was for sure thankful for the food arriving before she lost her mind and her chastity with the dark-haired bachelor. Now the mission was to contain herself until the safety of her apartment.

Meaning, no touchy-touchy naughty-naughty stuff with the bad boy.

All the way home.

In the car's confined space.

Eve pouted, she always had a thing for sex in cars, who knows why. At the sound of a soft chuckle at her side, she glanced sideways. Cyrus held her gaze, his eyes sparkling with a teasing light, sending a shiver down her spine as they waited for the lift to take them down to the ground floor.

Damn it.

The realisation hit her, the elevator. Two confined spaces she needed to hold back from jumping on the man and begging him to fuck her. And he was not going to help her stay respectable. Her pulse quickened as the lift finally landed, opening its door to hell. As soon as they entered, the air between them grew thick, her fingers twitching slightly, pulling on her dress as she fought the urge to reach out and touch his skin. She glanced quickly at Cyrus, who was looking at her hands, still clenching, the smile on his face calling for trouble.

"What?" she muttered, distracted a fraction of a second by the group of three businessmen entering the lift before the doors slid back, forcing the couple to back up a bit.

Cyrus went straight to the back of the lift pulling her against him, holding her butt against his thighs. Her gasp had the other group of people peering at her and in return she whispered a high pitch "Good eveniiing" which ended with Cyrus holding back his laugh. His torso silently moving up and down, in an effort to contain his usually gigantic laugh.

She gave him a sharp elbow, certain he would barely feel it. In return, the only thing she could feel while the lift was FINALLY going down, was Cyrus hardening against her ass.

The lift stopped at another floor, and Eve held back her breath as Cyrus's hand started its way down the line of her back. Great.

I mean, who doesn't like a back rub, this is fine.

Enjoying the caress more than she should, she gave in, his warm and huge hand alternating between a light caress and a full massage, but soon his hand went lower. If someone looked at her face right now, they would guess something was wrong. Her eyes betrayed her, her cheeks were burning, and her lips felt dry.

His hand was starting to adventure lower now, MUCH lower, patting her round ass, lifting up her dress.

Another stop. Another floor. People going in and out. And soon, a finger was going in and out.

Eve caught Cyrus's hand in hers, holding it tight against her stomach, while she subtly spread her legs, giving him better access, letting him play. It didn't take long before she could feel her juices all over the place, savouring his enormous and expert fingers teasing her, everywhere and nowhere at the same time. Up and down her slit, all the way up to push on her sensitive button, then when she could barely breathe, leaving it, heading back to her drenched slit, to finally entering her. One finger, two fingers. She wouldn't be able to stay quiet if he went to three. Her fingers gripped his hand harder, and she turned her head lightly to look at him, a storm in his eyes staring at her, continuing his back and forth downstairs.

She was so close to an orgasm but before she could release his fingers left, stopping their dance. At Eve's speechless look, the man smiled, quickly pulled her dress back and pushed her forward lightly towards the exit.

"We're down love" he murmured, guiding her shaking body, frustrated and wet, oh so wet.

"I fucking hate you!" She slapped his hand once out of the lift, getting a few curious looks from people waiting in the lobby.

"You didn't seem to hate me that much ten seconds ago," Cyrus laughed, catching up with her, as she walked angrily towards the glass doors, deciding to call a cab to teach him a lesson. Once outside, Cyrus on her heels, laughing in the background — *asshole!* — she took her phone out and he caught her hand and in a swift movement blocking her arms behind her back, all while carrying her to the shadows of one of the gigantic columns of the entrance.

He pressed her against the marble, and she welcomed the cold texture against her burning skin. Cyrus was still holding her hands, standing above her at a worrying altitude.

"Spread your legs." His voice was raspy and Eve couldn't believe it but it was even sexier than before.

"No."

"That was not a request Genevieve," he whispered in her ear, making her tremble under the words, placing his knee between her legs, pushing them apart, daring to chuckle at the whine escaping her.

Before she could protest again, his fingers started back right where they stopped before.

Oh well, I will teach him a lesson next time.

Rage.

Hate.

Disgust.

There aren't enough words to describe the scene a few metres away. At least not nice ones.

This fucking little whore. She was MINE.

MINE.

MINE.

Hands clench in a rageful fist, the pain of my nails digging in the chair doesn't matter. My eyes can't let go of the porn action on display, it's dark under the columns but I would recognise her anywhere. That hair, those fucking legs I would rip open, that mouth.

She's with Cyrus, I knew I needed to keep an eye on her. She's just like all the others. Just a fucking whore that deserves to die.

A sigh lingers on the air, hanging on a hope for a second she didn't hear me, but she's too busy being fingerfucked by the bastard.

Now is not the time to lose my mind.

Time to get ready for the next step.

Death.

Chapter 8

Eve

Eve was busy spreading her favourite cream on her legs, savouring the familiar ritual and the lavender smell, only to have her peaceful moment disturbed by the ring of her phone. With a mixture of annoyance and excitement she read the name on the screen. Cyrus.

She sighed, twisting her lips into a conflicted grimace, playing the game of seduction while hiding her passion for murder would be a bit tricky to handle. But to her demise, there was something in Cyrus that drew her in. "You mean besides his biceps and that tight little ass?" she spoke to herself; the man was for sure a treat for the eyes. Not to mention how agile his fingers were.

She grabbed the phone quickly before it stopped ringing, no way she would call him back on her own.

"Allo?" she tried to answer in a detached voice.

"Hello my beautiful Goddess." Cyrus's voice resonated in the phone. "I'm taking you to the Opera in two weeks, next Saturday. Book your evening."

Eve rolled her eyes, she wasn't sure if she should feel flattered that Cyrus wanted to see her again, or worried. But the thought of his hands on her body... And weirdly enough, the evening had been quite pleasant. Her mind quickly went to Erik, and how much trouble she could be creating for both of them.

"Hello? Did I lose you?" the deep voice interrupted her hesitation.

"No no, I was thinking," Eve replied, gathering her thoughts. "And perhaps, you know, expecting some kind of politeness, like basics stuff, 'how are you?' 'please?' 'thank you Goddess of my heart.' You know Cyrus, the kind of words civilised people say on the phone when inviting someone."

She had to move the phone away from her ear when Cyrus's thunderous laughter echoed in her now-deaf ear.

At least he thinks I'm funny.

"Darling, sorry, I'm used to getting what I want... So? Opera? Saturday night, next week?"

She laughed slightly; Cyrus was Cyrus after all.

"Which one?" She did love Opera, and who didn't love the beautiful dress and the occasion to get out of the house for something other than murders.

"The Traviata. That's..."

"I know what it is. Unfortunately for you, I'm not as stupid as your usual conquests."

Cyrus laughed again. "You mean luckily for me."

Eve blushed like an enamoured teenager, and she glanced at her reflection in the mirror witnessing it, the shame of the girly-girl-oh-my-god-he-is-so-hot. Her cheeks were red and glowing under the light, this was not good at all. But the Traviata had always held a special place in her heart, God knows why, because it was rather depressing.

"Yes."

"Excellent. Just a detail." There was mischief in his voice.

"Yes?" Eve had come to expect the worst when it came to Cyrus.

"Even though I loved your outfit from the other night, I don't think my sanity can handle a second date with you dressed like that. Try something less seductive... unless of course you enjoyed our sweet moment at the restaurant... and in the lift. And outside."

Man he was good, here she was again, on fire, the bare memories of his fingers teasing her were just enough to light her.

"Well, I'll take out my pyjamas and unicorn slippers."

"Perfect, we will make the pages of the magazines I'm sure," Cyrus laughed.

"I'd rather not." The last thing she needed was her picture in the tabloids. He laughed again, causing Eve to raise her voice to be heard over him.

"I will see you then Cyrus, properly dressed and all, have a good day. Don't come and annoy me at the station." She hung up before he had time to say anything, hoping her tone would be enough to convince the man not to come by.

A frustrated groan emerged from her throat; she was already regretting her decision to give in to temptation. Showing up with Cyrus was not the brightest idea of the century, maybe not even of the year, but it was so difficult to resist him.

Not to mention he wouldn't take no for an answer anyway, soooo she may as well deal with it, right?

Eve's thought drifted towards the serial killer wreaking havoc in Dublin. Not herself, the psychopath. The one killing innocent women. Eve had never considered herself a psychopath and she never killed women.

She was now pretty certain Cyrus had nothing to do with the killer. She could feel it from the beginning, but just in case, had kept a little doubt in her, after all one can never be too careful.

Maybe she should give up her own nocturnal activities for a while, let the police search for the killer and forget about her pieces of art. Her Guild wanted her to lie low for a while anyway, still growling at her about "discretion." The Guild had learned about the slashed penis, and was not happy about it. Even if there were no witnesses.

"Discretion blehblebleh," Eve mumbled, finishing her beauty ritual while cursing her Guild and their boring rules. That's when it hit her. She stopped breathing, straightening herself she talked to her reflection.

"Oooor, even better, maybe I should try to find the psychopath first." She laughed with excitement, standing up, after all he was the pinnacle of what she was fighting. And with Cyrus's help and means she could surely find him faster. Eve placed the pot of cream down and grimaced, it wasn't her favourite solution, but this guy had to be stopped. Sighing, she stretched her legs, their once bronzed complexion now faded to blend in with Ireland, and made her way to her computer, determined to investigate.

The sound of an incoming message on her phone stopped her. She sighed, certain it was Cyrus, either saying something naughty, or better, sending some naughty pics. Catching her annoying device nonchalantly, her face froze as she read the message from the giant.

"Btw, there was another murder, I'm sure you're gonna get busy at work so if you feel like you need to release some tension… I'm your man."

First, how amazing was it that someone like Cyrus used emojis? Second, for fuck's sake, another murder? He didn't need to give details, she guessed it was a murder from the psychopath, the only thing she could hope was that this time her colleagues would get some clues. And let's be crazy, maybe the acknowledgement from their superior about the whole serial killer situation.

The thought of Cyrus knowing before her was disturbing, especially seeing he was still kind of the prime suspect. But then from what she understood, he was also responsible for many secret pay-checks in the department.

It was with a fearless and decided step that Eve entered the police station the next morning. It was only mid-week but the last few days had become somewhat irritable and rumours at the station were running wild about Cyrus's possible involvement. Eve didn't really care about those rumours though.

Cyrus was big enough to take care of those accusations himself, as long as they didn't interfere in her nocturnal activities. Including her possible future date with the Golden Boy.

Upon entering the main room, she felt cold, hair on her arm spiking. *Something's going on for sure.* She had hoped the new murder was something entirely new, mostly because she hated when Cyrus was right, and that he knew before her. She spotted Erik, Andy, Bonnie, and Mark, who was eyeing her bottom as often as he could. They stopped the conversation as she approached and she raised an interrogative eyebrow towards Erik without a word. Erik put his hand over his face, she knew this gesture having seen it unfortunately twice already, and she knew what it preceded.

"There was another murder." Eric's usual happy wrinkles at the corner of his eyes were not showing today, and for one second Eve found him old.

"Obviously." She shook her head.

At the suspicious glances and questioning eyes, she reacted fast. "I mean, just look at your faces."

Erik coughed and raised his voice to address the whole team on the floor. "Everyone in the meeting room now!"

Everyone grabbed notepads and coffee before heading for the meeting room. Eve settled in her favourite corner, the one where she could look at everyone and watch the front door, habit. She crossed her legs, adjusted her skirt, and got ready to take notes for her future minute report.

Erik started. "It's official, we have a third murder on our backs."

Angry murmurs ran through the room, before the boss could put a stop to it.

"I know, I know," he calmed in a loud voice, his hands in the air as if he was taming a wild animal. "But good news is we finally have permission from our gentlemen superiors to open a special investigation for this serial killer."

Murmurs of approval replaced the growls, many nodding. Bonnie especially had closed her eyes, a smile so faint on her lips you could barely guess it was there.

Erik turned to his computer, his fingers flying over the keyboard. He clicked a few buttons, way too slowly for Eve's taste, and the photos of the new body materialised on the white screen in front of the group. As the images appeared, a mixture of reactions spread throughout the room. Some turned their heads away, unable to watch, while others casted their looks towards their notepads. Eve, however, always confronted the brutality, forcing herself to look, reminding herself why she had chosen her particular hobby.

"The body was discovered yesterday evening by a bunch of kids, hidden amidst the garbage cans, two streets away from the previous one." Erik clicked another button scrolling through the horrors on the screen.

"The victim has been identified as 30-year-old Emily Stones, barmaid."

What looked like a recent photograph of Emily appeared, captivating the room. A beautiful woman, a delicate face, her raven dark hair was almost as long as Eves and a little wavy, and topping it all off, hypnotising green eyes. Eve felt the anger in her rising. *One more victim to the madness of men.* It reaffirmed her decision to involve herself in this shit one way or another. The guy was like her, he was enjoying it, and he would never stop.

"Irishtown," someone whispered, enticing more murmurs throughout the room. *Cyrus's neighbourhood.* Eve grimaced.

Johnny, the fish looking guy scoffed. "The killer must be living in the neighbourhood huh?"

To Eve's great pleasure, Erik held back a sigh. "Not especially, he may well have chosen a place he knows without necessarily living there."

"Or just because it's convenient," Eve added, thinking out loud while clicking on her pen too many times. Heads turned. She sure hoped she didn't look like a deer in headlights right now, eyes wide open, frozen.

"Proximity to his workplace, or to some warehouse or garage he has access to. A place where he can keep them alive... you know, for a few days." She shrugged.

The weight of the looks on her made her panic a tiny bit more. "I happen to live in this neighbourhood and the small alleys are so dark they are perfect to dispose of a body."

Silence.

"Not that I know anything about dropping bodies in the wild," she hastily added with a smile she hoped looked innocent.

The policemen exchanged glances, and Eve rolled her eyes feigning nonchalance, pretending to return to her notes.

Eric cleared his throat. "Thank you, Eve, for the intervention," he said, giving her big eyes. Turning, he addressed the room. "Andy and Bonnie, you're in charge. Take all the files we have and METICULOUSLY review all of them."

The Duo nodded.

"Joy, and Isabelle, you've already worked on some of these murders so you're part of the team. A closed knit team. Hear my emphasis on the closed here? I'm already going to have the press on my back so let's give them nothing but the bare minimum. No leaks. No talking about the case outside of this station. Clear?"

A few nods of approval followed, enticing Eric to continue.

"Mark, I know you're on the Saviour, but if the team needs you, you're on call."

Mark grumbled but didn't dare protest out loud.

Erik continued. "Our primary focus is to find a common point between our victims. We need to know how the hell he picks them."

He sighed. "Eve, I would like you to contact Ian Rocfield"

Eve's eyes widened.

"He's the only profiler in Ireland, we need him. Thankfully he's good at it." Before Eve could say what she thought about this, terrible, terrible, terrible, idea Andy spoke up.

"Erik? Seriously? Ian? We're gonna have freaking McRory on our backs already, we don't need his best friend hanging out around here." A few murmurs of agreement ran through the room but were quickly silenced by Erik's firm voice.

"There is no discussion to have, we are running around like headless chickens. We NEED this profile, we need someone with new eyes." He sighed, this particular point was going to be tough. "Besides, I have worked with Ian in the past, before the war. He is pretty good at separating his work and his... attachment to Cyrus."

Eve pulled a face, even though Ian seemed quite serious compared to, well, Cyrus, she didn't see how he could stop the giant reading through all the files. But maybe he had more will than she did to resist the Golden Boy's charms.

Erik continued. "Room number 3 on my floor, only the people whose names I just mentioned are allowed access. Clear? If necessary, we will extend the team."

Nobody said a word, but everyone knew. They'll expand the team once another murder or two was committed.

Eric paused. "I know you are all worried about Cyrus sniffing around. I am asking you to please trust me, I will have a talk with Ian myself."

He was more talking to himself than the room when he muttered, "I'm gonna try to distract Cyrus on the Saviour instead... keep him busy...".

Erik stopped his look turning to Eve and she could not stop the blush reaching her cheeks, quickly burring her head in her notes. Having Cyrus on her back was the last of her wishes. Having him on his back though, ideally naked while she could mount him, now that was another story.

"Please make sure you don't leave anything lying around, you all know Cyrus," he sighed. Some nodded, others grumbled, Andy whispered "sneaky son of a bitch."

Eve nodded lost in her thoughts of a naked Cyrus answering all of her desires. His body pushing her against a wall, his fingers rising dangerously towards her warm entrance... She bit her lip, trying to focus.

"We know very well he will get his hands on information, so we have to be careful. Especially if you see Zorfield hanging around, that one is a freaking sneaky one. Let's not put our killer in Cyrus's hands." Erik levelled them all with a glare.

Mark grumbled. "For once I'll agree to let him do it." Murmurs of approval rose in the room.

Erik shook his head. "We represent justice, we cannot afford to let him do his own justice. Clear?"

Eve laughed internally. *Erik really loves the word "Clear?"*

Johnny, the pervert fish, rose his hand to speak. "But chief, should we not investigate Cyrus? After all, the murders were in his neighbourhood, weren't they? Commander Cragnum wanted us to look into it."

A few laughs emanated in the room as Eve's disgust for the pervert fish deepened, perhaps because his gaze on her had thickened, he just did the irreparable, already replacing Erik as Commander.

"After all, he knew the first two," Johnny continued. "I bet you he knew this one too, he has the means to attract these women, not to mention enough power to silence us. That's all I'm saying."

That was the most ridiculous theory Eve had ever heard. Not only was Johnny ugly, but he was stupid as well. No wonder he was jealous of her Cyrus.

Erik held out his hand. "The women were abducted from their homes, with evidence of them putting up a fight."

"Do you know many women who would resist Cyrus Fucking McRory?" Andy looked to Johnny and Eve realised in that moment he had no fondness for Johnny either. She made a mental note to ask Bonnie about the reason why Andy was so anti-Cyrus.

"Interesting theory Johnny" Erik said.

"Or not," Eve muttered, starting to scribble a grouper amid her notes.

"But having known Cyrus since birth, I can assure you he is many things, but certainly not a rapist, or a murderer... Of women." He cleared his throat, everyone knew the McRory son didn't mind a kill or two from time to time, he was a gang leader after all. "Keep an open mind, yes, check his alibis, check his... acquaintances of those women, but I would rather us not lose our time on him."

Not a rapist, good to know. Though she kind of knew that already.

As the officers prepared to leave, Erik spoke. "By the way, don't forget we have the Gala this Saturday."

Grumbles and protests erupted from various corners of the room, this time getting everyone to agree.

Erik raised his hand to stop the movement. "I know, I know! But it would be appreciated if most of you could attend, and be on your best behaviour, and absolutely no getting drunk!"

A moment of silence followed, broken once more by Erik. "Clear?"

Eve had completely forgotten about the Gala. She realised with anticipation she would need to buy a new dress. The sexy one she was planning to buy for her date with Cyrus to the Opera might be a bit too revealing for a charity event.

Chapter 9

Cyrus

Away from the bustling city centre and Eve's hassle, Cyrus was lost in thought. He had found out about the newly found body before everyone thanks to his contacts at the station, and would soon have Ian's confirmation that he had fucked this girl too, a while ago.

And a fool was trying to blame him for the crimes, driving Erik to look into him for the sake of it. These imbeciles would never understand him.

But knowing the cunning nature of Lois nothing could be left to chance, the man was probably trying to cause trouble behind the scenes, pushing the actual Commander to act. Cyrus had a genuine appreciation for Erik, and he didn't want to embarrass him before his retirement, which he thoroughly deserved. Which meant he had a few weeks to conquer his new target — Eve.

She was driving him crazy, and he was fully aware of it. He had high hopes for the night before and was not planning to be left at the door of the building like a virgin with blue balls as soon as he gave her back her necklace.

Cyrus was not known to be a man of patience, in anything, which, now that he thought about it, might be the reason he was in trouble. Three women, three ex-conquests, three one-night stands. Unlike Eve, they didn't reject him for a good night of fun.

At first it had been more of a game, the girl was attractive. But what truly captivated him was her perpetual indignant gaze and her resistance. Cyrus sighed; he was such a cliché. He stood by the window observing his two friends frolicking in the park adjacent to their house. Cyrus wasn't used to being resisted. Man, woman, banker, restaurateur... Everyone said yes to Cyrus McRory. Out of respect. Or fear.

But she was stubborn! Ian found it absolutely hilarious and loved telling his lover about the office scene.

Their intimate time at the restaurant at least made him feel confident he would get to her after all. *Her hardened nipples and her drenched pussy...* He felt himself getting tight again in his jeans.

His two best friends had already made bets on whether he would end up fucking the beautiful French. Ian, the traitor, thought she was playing with him and that she probably wouldn't give it up again. Zorfied, his true best friend, was quite confident in Cyrus's skills.

Ian even went to the extent to give Cyrus advice. ADVICE! From a gay man who has only had one lover ever in his life. *"Don't do anything you would normally do with your other conquests."*

Cyrus shook his head. He never had trouble getting a damn girl before, either his body or his money always helped. But Eve apparently didn't care about his money. Though, he was pretty sure he had seen her looking at his butt on their date.

"Behave and don't be pushy." This last point would be the hardest since Cyrus only had one desire, pushing Eve against a wall and taking off her clothes. His pants got even tighter remembering the low backline she wore Saturday night.

Cyrus let out a sigh, adjusted his pants, and decided to visit his friends to distract himself. Before leaving, he grabbed his phone and composed a message to Eve.

All things considered, a dress showing more of this amazing breast of yours should do the trick.

The answer came back swiftly — a selfie of the young woman sticking her tongue. Cyrus chuckled, at least she had a sense of humour.

Eve

Back at the police station, Eve set down her phone, glancing around to see if anyone had seen her, even though she was alone in her office. Aware that playing the game of cat and mouse with the bad boy would get her into trouble. She sighed trying to focus on her work, connecting to the police resource to find Ian's professional contact. After the war, and for obscure reasons, it was decided the police forces could no longer exchange profilers. The various conspiracies and collaborations had made the different countries totally paranoid. In Ireland, the problem was that there was only one left alive.

Eve would never have guessed that this sweet and discreet character was a talented profiler. There was a good chance he'd tell Cyrus all the details, even if Erik made it clear he could not. At least he seemed to have his head on his shoulders, compared to Cyrus or Zorfield.

Five minutes later, after a quick call to Ian, and trying to not pay attention to Cyrus's loud laugh in the background, she was quite happy. Eve pushed her chair and headed to room 3, where the team was reconstructing the murders from the beginning. A huge white board with tons of photos and comments was starting to take place. *Probably trying to find the famous common ground.*

Some lived literally two streets next to Eve's. Anyone else would freak out, but Eve thought it was more annoying that this killer was so close to her home. *Sorry boy, there's only room for one crazy killer in this town.*

She came into the room without knocking, heads raising up at her entrance, before falling back when they saw it was her. She should be used to this, as a rather cute woman she had always had two reactions. People either thought she was a lovely idiot, or they thought she was a lovely and easy idiot. At the police station, it was option one. Most didn't really know why Erik hired her and there had been rumours about them, which quickly stopped when they saw Eve hugging Erik's wife.

Erik spotted her and after quickly finishing his conversation with Bonnie, walked over.

He sighed. "Come on, swing."

"Ian has gladly accepted to work on the cases, he is aware of the... um... problems, his relationship with Cyrus could cause and is more than happy to work only at the station with no files or info coming out."

She took a quick breath while Erik glanced at the inspectors, who were acting as if they were not listening. But were.

"Thank you Eve," Erik sighed. "Let's see how it goes."

Eve smiled to her friend and was going to leave the room, leaving them to their work, when Erik stopped her, a hand on her arm. She turned to him, surprised.

"When Ian is around, and if Cyrus is sneaking in here too, try not to get on his path eh?" Erik was looking at her behind his glasses, a concerned look on his face. Eve held back a scoff, glad he had no idea about her naughty behaviour.

"Of course."

She smiled, trying to take a quick last look at the white board behind Erik before leaving but didn't want to look too obvious. She should think about getting better at espionage though, because she was next on the list of serial killers to find.

Sitting back at her desk, she read Cyrus's message again, and with a heavy guilt she decided to play.

Cyrus

Cyrus looked down at his phone when another text came through, interrupting his suspicion of Ian, who had been acting weird since he received a call. Zorfield didn't seem to be bothered about it, but then, it was Zorfield, he didn't bother about much anyway, Cyrus was much more paranoid.

A snarly smile spread when he saw Eve's name and opened the video she sent. He scoffed at the view of her fingers, pulling at her nipple, playing around her breast, squeezing it, making him want to be the one to play with her body. A growl escaped him when the video stopped, deciding to play it again, and again.

His friends could make fun of him as much as they wanted, he was going to get the girl.

And she is going to scream my name.

Chapter 10

Eve

Eve told herself she wouldn't do it. She said she would behave.

Oh well.

With a sigh, she raised her hands to slightly adjust her new acquisition: a white mask with two hollow spaces for her eyes. It was the kind of thing you wear to a horror movie marathon, or at Halloween. Not to wait for some drunken loser in a sketchy neighbourhood at midnight. It also wasn't the comfiest thing she'd ever worn, but it did the job. After her previous mistake with the 11's, she could not afford any potential witnesses even spotting a bit of skin, so here she was, playing ghostface while stalking her new suspect.

Potential suspect. She had no proof whatsoever of his role as the psychopath, but the police considered this guy's name important enough to place it at the top on the anti-psycho team whiteboard at the station. Jody was apparently well known as a sex offender before the war, and even though he didn't torture or kill his victims then, he received a diagnostic of PTSD following his war days. Eve knew way too well what war could do to you, so here she was, alternating between standing, stretching, and kneeling, in the darkest corner she could find in this sad neighbourhood.

Jody had been hanging out in the same pub for the past four freaking hours, and there was only so much she could take. Any other day she would have waited patiently for him in his house, like she usually did, but if this guy was the killer there was no way she would take the risk of letting him hurt another girl just because Eve was feeling lazy. That said, the longer she stayed here, the more she thought there was no way the guy could get it up enough to rape a girl tonight.

Shaking her leg, ankylosed, she thought about her plan. It was basic, and quite bad. Wait for him, follow him, get into his house, make him talk.

Psychopath? Great, he can die. Not a psychopath? Well, technically speaking, he was still a rapist anyway, so death was still on the menu.

A quick thought brushed her mind. She told her Guild she would not go on any mission right now, just taking a breather, letting the whole "serial killer" business cool down for a bit. But what the Guild didn't know could not hurt them, right?

If they learn about this, I'm in such deep shit.

Eve groaned in her dark corner. She had spent the past two days sneaking around the anti-psycho team, being the perfect little secretary, offering coffee to the tired detectives while eyeing their files and notes. The team was at a loss, but they had pulled a few names from old files and added some information on the board, enticing Eve to read them. She had duly noted the names and decided to check her favourite profile for a potential serial killer. And now here she was, waiting in the cold, feeling like an absolute idiot. On a Thursday night. Cyrus had offered her a visit, promising her a massage, and she had refused because of her plans to catch and torture Jody. She was now regretting her decision.

Regret quickly left when she saw him, a hesitant, stumbling man, recognising the red cap he was wearing when he went in, now looking as if it would not stay on his dishevelled head for long.

"Finally," she muttered, and checking her mask a last time she got ready to follow him. White mask and hoodie, how about this for discretion?

The man was walking painfully slow, thankfully heading towards his street, located only 300meters or so from his favourite pub. Eve was losing patience with the snail speed of Jody, the guy was so drunk he was taking one step forward and two steps backwards, and she was so done with it. Eve rolled her eyes. She glanced around and took off her mask, enjoying the fresh air on her skin. She inhaled deeply, buried the mask in her bag, and crossed the street, keeping her hoodie over her head.

"Hey bud, you need a hand?" she spoke fast, trying to hide her strong accent, then gave him the smile she knew would get her anything she wanted with men.

Blurry eyes met hers, blinking. She caught him quickly as his body dangerously started falling to his left side.

"Imdrunk,"

"Yeah no kidding," Eve mumbled. She placed her arm behind him, guiding him towards his flat. She had done her research and knew exactly where to go, hoping he didn't lose his keys. She scanned the street, a few walkers were strolling across the way but nobody was paying attention to them, who from far enough away looked like two pretty drunk friends.

As they finally reached his flat, Jody fumbled for his keys, struggling to reach in his pockets.

Eve stood there, tapping her foot. *I am so not going into your pocket guy.* She pouted, very much rather wanting to head straight to the bloody part of the evening.

Once the toughest part of the evening was done - opening the freaking door - the couple entered the dirty, smelly flat. Eve had to control the disgust coming at her, wincing her nose at the smell; her soft side wanted to understand how hard it could be to take care of yourself. Her not-so-nice side could just not get it.

She puffed dropping him on the first chair she found, and when he tried to aim for the couch instead she went full mode secret agent: blocking his neck, pushing hard on his throat, barely listening to the muffled screams, ignoring the hands trying to reach her. With her other hand she quickly caught one of his arms, snapping a handcuff on his wrist, before the other one. He was way too drunk to resist her, and it was with a silent resignation he started crying.

Eve rolled her eyes, and moved in front of him, her mask back on.

"Jody. Jody?" She snapped her fingers at his face when he didn't answer, instead still crying, his sad head bent over his chest.

"This can go fast, or slow." She kneeled close to his eye level. The prisoner finally raised his head, eyes blurry, snot coming out of his nose.

"What do you want?"

"Did you kill them?" Eve showed him three pictures. Roisin, Mary and Emily, all young and beautiful, all smiling. Jody blinked his eyes a few times, taking his time to look at the pictures.

"No, I have killed no one since the war, I swear." He took a deep inhale and tipped his head backwards, as if relieved.

"Can you prove it?"

"I don't need to prove anything to you, bitch!" he spat at her, and it was his mistake.

Eve scoffed, glad the spit had landed on her new mask instead of her pretty smooth skin.

"Then you won't mind if I make sure of it?"

Jody's blue eyes were still hazed by the alcohol and he didn't answer, his head bouncing from side to side, as if he couldn't control it. When he saw Eve's knife, he opened his mouth, ready to scream, but she was faster, quickly introducing a ball in his mouth, shutting him off. That's when she started to cut.

Chapter 11

Eve

The next morning, Eve walked into the police station with the biggest smile on her face. Not only was she wearing a new dress - that made a girl happy - but she also had a new trophy at home. Last night's fun with Jody had left her with a peculiar sense of accomplishment, and helped release some of her accumulated tension. Her day job was so stressful, after all.

Unfortunately Jody wasn't the psychopath she was hoping for, but knowing all the shady things he'd done over the years, Eve figured he might as well be dead. As far as she was concerned, he perfectly fit her conditions for a good slaughter. Yes, she had criteria.

She practically skipped towards her office, ready for a good day of crime-solving. Or at least a good day of sneaking around, making coffee, and sending naughty pictures to Cyrus. Add a good fuck to this day, and it would be perfect. She immediately stopped all thoughts of fucking when she spotted Johnny, following her with his insipid look, she ignored him. Not today. She was feeling way too good for paying attention to him.

Her good mood didn't last long, though. Andy caught up with her, bearer of bad news.

"Hey girl, you seem happy," he said, raising an eyebrow.

"And you don't," Eve retorted.

He grunted. "Yeah, we have a body, one of our suspects." He whispered the last words to her, but that made Eve stop her giddy walk, her eyes wide open.

"Really?" she asked, hysteria in her voice. Damn it, she knew she should have hidden the body. But there was no way she could have done that without being spotted. She was at least hoping for two or three days before someone found him, she had turned on all the heaters in the tiny flat, knowing it would mess up the body a bit before being found. *I should have burned the fucking building to the ground.*

Andy didn't seem to be shocked by her reaction and continued, gripping the file he had in his hands. "Yeah, and he didn't have a good end, I can tell you that. He was tortured for sure, they even cut his d..." he stopped abruptly, certainly remembering who he was talking too. Eve was silent, trying to get a hold of her insides panicking.

"Anyway, better go." Andy saw something above Eve's shoulder and nodded his head. "Hey Mark, where the fuck you running? We have a body."

She heard Mark's footsteps before she saw him, glancing just in time to see him pass by, his coat on his arm, walking fast towards the exit. Not breaking his stride. "Nope, got a lead on the 11's killer," he said with a grin, a grin that said this could be good.

For him. Not for her.

Eve froze watching Mark run out the door, her stomach did a full backflip, followed by a spin, then a complete drop. Where had her perfect day gone? She was stuck. Both Andy and Mark? Both bad omens for her day.

She couldn't follow Mark without being questioned, so she might as well head up to the anti-psycho team and cross all her fingers and toes that nothing could lead to her. *I'm so glad I bought a mask.*

Eve quickly went to drop her jacket in her office before heading to the anti-psycho room. She arrived, giving her usual smile to the team. None really noticed her, too busy looking at the new pictures on the new whiteboard.

Pictures of her artwork from last night.

Eeeek, I did that?

She didn't even bother trying to hide, going straight to the board, standing beside Bonnie who was mumbling a mix of English and Spanish swear words. Eve tried the best she could to hold back a smile. He did have it coming. Jody was a rapist, with paedophiles tendencies, nothing people should cry about. Ok, he was now missing his dick, and his nails had all been torn off, but she had to make sure he was telling the truth. It's not her fault it took ten nails before finally accepting Jody's talk as it was: he was innocent, and not her nemesis.

"She got him good."

Eve felt her eyes jump out of their orbits as she turned towards Erik, his rectangular glasses showing some blur on the bottom, proof he had rushed here. She didn't say a word, hoping someone would jump on it before she did, but after a few seconds, she had to accept the fact that nobody was going to help her.

"Her?" Eve asked, her voice as chill as she could keep it.

Erik nodded, and looked at her, as if wondering what she was doing here, looking at their boards.

"Yes, a witness thinks he was with a woman."

"Ouch, bad date, uh?"

On her side, she felt Andy jump, scoffing. "That shit was not a date girl, look at him. I say that's our freaking killer. The slashed peen, maybe even the 11's." He was mumbling, as if talking to himself, already imagining the possibilities.

"Or a copycat." Bonnie turned away from the pictures and headed to her desk. "I think we need to keep in mind that this killer might give ideas to some people. And Jody had a sexual offender file, same as the slashed peen."

"And now he is out of a dick too." Andy smiled.

Eve wondered for one second if she should intervene, maybe give them the idea that the guy was also at the top of their list.

"Jody was one of our suspects in the serial killer case." Erik sighed. "We need to imagine the possibility that's what got him killed."

Bonnie turned towards her Commander. "You think someone wanted to get to him before us?" She seemed to think about it as Erik nodded his head. "Then that means whoever we have on our suspect list needs protection, Erik."

Andy slouched in his chair, a finger in the air. "That's Cyrus Freaking McRory right there! He must have spied on us, took down the names, and went for a hunt to look for the killer himself."

Eve, who was sitting at Andy's desk, holding back a smirk, wondered if she should bury Cyrus or not. Couldn't hurt to have some fun after all. She gasped. "My God, Andy, you think so?"

Andy, happy for someone to finally listen to him, nodded, and was probably ready to enter a full-length description of why he thought Cyrus was the culprit when Erik stopped him.

"Enough. We keep as it is. Eve, back to your office, you are not needed right now. Andy, as I said, we keep an open mind. I agree this murder could go both ways, either it's our 11's killer, or someone who thought he was our serial killer."

Andy stayed silent for two seconds.

"Does that mean I can look into Cyrus?"

Erik sighed rubbing his temples. "Yes. Yes, you can."

Eve almost laughed. Poor Cyrus, but better him than her. Erik threw her a look, it was time for her to leave, so she jumped out of the room, leaving the team to their tasks.

Chapter 12

Eve

All together it had been a hectic second half of a week, and besides her quick murder Thursday night, Eve had been busy with the investigation, giving help in whatever research or coffee-making she was required for the last few days. Anything to give her a chance to glance at the whiteboard, not that she would be able to do anything about it. They had placed policemen to watch two potential suspects, both sexual offenders. Which stopped her going and have fun, but she had no doubt either was the serial killer she was looking for anyway. Her detective skills had reached their limits, which to be honest were quite low to start with.

Thankfully, Ian was to start working on Monday, and he had seemed, for now, to have kept his promise to keep his future involvement as far away from Cyrus as possible. Eve had no doubt as soon as Cyrus knew she would hear an earful of it. Of course, the psycho-team wasn't happy about it, but they'd get used to it, it was hard to resist the charismatic redhead.

As for Eve, she was quite glad to have Ian around soon, and more than happy to let him do all the searching-and-looking work, she just wanted to do the slash-slash-kill part.

What was the point in doing hard detective work really?

Like poor Mark, who came back empty handed from what was supposed to be an amazing clue about her. Turned out it was just a grumpy dumped boyfriend, accusing his ex. Truth be told, Eve could still not believe how good she had it with this 11's. None of the girls had talked or given any kind of useful information to the police. But they could not be stopped talking about the men who abused them during months, or years for some.

Girl power right there.

Letting out a sigh, she pushed open the door to the terrace of the magnificent castle where the Police Gala was taking place. This place was truly enchanting, radiating old legends and magic. But damn she hated these kinds of evenings. She promised Erik she would attend and besides, she heard rumours Cyrus and his friends usually showed up, taunting the police. Not that she was particularly keen on her colleagues discovering any connection between her and Cyrus. They exchanged texts, pictures, videos, and even a few phone calls the last three days, and she was burning for him. No longer sure how much she could hold back if left alone with him.

She was to blame for the exchanges, she was the one who started it with her naughty video, but she sure loved the long, intense, and detailed video of him wanking himself he sent as a prompt answer. She should have hated that kind of thing, because really, a dick video? But the man was well mounted and had a pretty dick. She couldn't wait to have a taste.

Eve let out an upset rale, bending over the railing, talking to herself. "Here you are again, playing with fire." She took a deep breath, revelling the refreshing scent of the sea. *Finally some fresh air.* Quite a contrast to Dublin, she loved the city but nothing could compare to the peaceful countryside. She had managed to escape the mundane – and boring – talks of some policemen wives, and after strolling along many corridors had found a quiet room to hide and admire the view of the terrace.

Leaning forward slightly, she gazed down at the direct drop into the ocean, sending a shiver down her spine. It wasn't high, maybe 10 metres, with no rocks waiting for her. She had done worse jumps than this, in ill conditions. She stretched a smile, then proceeded to kick off her heels, leaving them in a corner. Slowly, she dragged her dress along her body, revealing her naked form under the moonlight, knowing – hoping — she was alone. Gracefully she climbed the railing and jumped into the depths below.

Cyrus

Cyrus hadn't moved when Eve came outside, she didn't see him and when she started taking off her dress, he genuinely thought it was meant for him.

Sighing, he shook his head, looking down to the white figure swimming against the waves, sometimes surrendering to their gentle pull. She knew what she was doing.

"She's insane," he whispered, worried about the potential danger as she swam towards the cliff. He watched her head towards the nearby beach and smiled. Then picked up her discarded clothes before making his way back into the house.

Eve

Eve swallowed a large gulp of air and dove back into the water, she felt at ease, free of everything. She let her body float, facing down toward the ocean's sand, her hair floating behind her, only the muffled sound of the waves around her. She swam, peaking her head out, analysing the distance to the nearby beach she spotted earlier, it should lead her back to the mansion. The challenge now was to discreetly return to the party, completely naked, and grab her dress.

Oh well, that won't be easy she giggled to herself, swallowing some salty water on the way, keeping an elegant breaststroke until she decided to judge the distance to the bottom with her foot. Foot touching the soft sand, she took a moment to catch her breath before walking towards the beach.

Finally out of the water, she wrung her hair taking out as much as water as she could. Her senses sharpened and her body froze, feeling a presence on the beach, barely visible under the moonlight. Her steps became hesitant, until she saw him unfolding a large white towel and what appeared to be her clothes on the ground next to him. A smile spread across her face as she walked calmly towards Cyrus, his burning eyes on her, not holding back, looking at her entire body.

Cyrus struggled to maintain a certain composure with her standing before him, beautifully naked. Not that he would turn his eyes away, enjoying the full shape of her body, taking his sweet time. He scoffed when Eve landed her full cold body against his, well, against the towel he was holding, and closed the towel over her back.

"Charming attention." Eve leaned against his strong body, taking all his warmth into her. It was indeed a bit chilly, and she hadn't thought that through. But she warmed at the feel of something against her stomach that was either a very big mobile, or a very big dick, and she sure hoped it was the latter.

Under the glimmer of the moon, she stared at him without fear, he, who frightened the entire country.

"Nothing charming about it. I'm just saving you the trouble of having to explain to that bunch of people what you are doing naked on the beach."

Really big guy?

A drop of Eve's hair slipped down her back, sending a shiver through her body. Taking her time, she loosened the towel wrapped around her and used it to dry a bit her hair, her body once again on display. With a smirk on her face, she glanced at the man standing before her.

The familiar, lingering gaze in his eyes was as always present. Cyrus McRory, police enemy number one, her biggest rival in the hunt for the psychopath. And potential future bed partner.

He turned away slowly, but before he took a step, he turned his head back to her. "I hope you're aware that no one else will see you naked, ever."

And just like that, Cyrus left.

Eve sneered, finally witnessing a human reaction from him, the guy was indeed a bit possessive, she might regret playing the cat and mouse game later. Lost in her own thoughts, she continued to gently wring her hair. The cool air gave her the shivers, prompting her to get dressed fast. She picked up her silver dress, beautiful with a delicate fabric, an elegant slit on the left leg and once again a deep back. After all, Cyrus seemed to appreciate her back, and there was no hurting anyone in teasing him a bit.

Cyrus

Stepping into the grand hall, all eyes turned towards Cyrus. He was used to it, had grown accustomed to since his childhood. He had cultivated this enigmatic aura surrounding him, leaving everyone to guess about his true nature. He was not a "good" guy, yet he was genuinely interested in the well-being of his neighbourhood, even the city. Not to mention he was a proud patriot. Rival gangs quickly learned that aligning with McRory was essential for their survival.

Cyrus returned to his friends, who had remained in the exact same place he left them earlier, whispering to each other. A smile appeared on his face when he saw them, the fact that his two friends were homosexual and openly displaying it from a young age had always made people gossip about Cyrus's own sexual orientation. Yet he had never been attracted to men. Women, on the other hand had been a source of great pleasure for him, indulging himself frequently, as the police noticed.

"Where were you?" Ian asked with a disapproving air, his red eyebrows narrowing over those icy blue eyes so characteristic of him.

Cyrus grabbed a glass of champagne from a waitress. "Why? Was there a murder? A revolution? Or perhaps some woman in dire need of my attention?"

Ian raised his eyes to the heavens, a gesture he had mastered to perfection. "Third option. Specifically, womEN, your dear step-mama has decided to pair you up with Tiphany. Who had her breasts done, just so you know."

Cyrus staggered, taking a sip of his champagne, not sure where this conversation was going. "What does her fake breasts have to do with Andrea's plans?" His step-mum had been trying since the end of the war to pair him with any heiress from good Irish blood, and he was done with it.

"Well," Ian started. "She's convinced that if you can't find anyone, it must be because you're too picky... and since Tiphany has a generous bosom now, she's convinced she'll be to your liking."

Cyrus finished his drink, holding back his laughter. Ian hated as much, if not more, all the pretentiousness displayed by the individuals present tonight. This charity event was the only one they usually attended. Not only for the pleasure of witnessing the disapproving looks from the police but also because Erik's wife happened to be a close friend of Cyrus's actual mother.

He spotted his step-mum whispering with Tiphany's mother... *So there is indeed a plot going on.*

Ian had an infallible instinct for it. Always able to protect Cyrus from his own exacerbated desires. As the crowd of plotting women cast puzzled glances behind him, a shiver ran through his body. Eve.

Tiphany, perhaps attempting a sardonic humour laughed. "It seems the French have strange manners after all." A sneer-and-giggle from all the ladies around her followed.

Eve approached the small group, arching an eyebrow, capturing the desperate, doe-eyed glances directed towards Cyrus. Unable to contain her smile, she turned, walking over to him.

"Good evening, Mr McRory," she purred in a falsetto voice, deliberately exaggerating her French accent.

Cyrus glanced at her, trying to hold back a smirk.

"Erik informed me you're intimately familiar with this charming mansion. I would simply ADORE it if you could give me a tour," Eve added, punctuating her statement with an ironic flicker.

"With pleasure." Cyrus smiled, extending his arm.

He swiftly turned towards his friends before walking out whispering, "I am more of a butt guy anyway".

Outraged glances pierced the couple as they strolled toward one of the grand double-doors, while his two friends laughed.

Chapter 13

Eve

Once they crossed the threshold, a sense of panic began to wash over Eve, realising she was once again putting herself in a vulnerable position with Cyrus. They encountered a few other couples along the sprawling corridors of the mansion. Some casted inquisitive glances their way, while others couldn't help but whisper as they passed, thankfully none of them colleagues she recognised.

Eve glanced at Cyrus, as discreetly as possible, the man donned in a midnight blue shirt and black leather pants. *Leather pants. To a gala.* Once again, the buttons on his fitted attire strained against his hairy torso, evoking a familiar warmth within Eve.

They seemed to wander aimlessly, until he gently tugged her hand, leading her into an expansive room that revealed itself as a breathtaking library. She couldn't help but widen her eyes in awe, beholding the sheer splendour of the place. Libraries had always held a special place in her heart, one could never have enough books.

The room was a sublime and vast space, adorned with towering walnut shelves reaching up to the ceiling. Mismatched yet comfortable couches were scattered throughout the room. In the centre stood an enormous round window, its height matching Cyrus's own stature, inviting the moonlight to flood the room. Eve's gaze darted around, searching for a light switch out of habit.

"Stop."

She remained silent as Cyrus's hands ventured over her breasts, a soft sigh escaping her as his fingers applied pressure, pinching her, sending waves of pleasure through her. She took a deep breath, allowing her head to lean back against his chest. The pinches became more intense, and Eve's breathing became jerky, her only desire for him to take her against the window. Cyrus released her breasts, prompting a grunt of protest from Eve, before gently sliding the thin straps of her dress off her shoulders.

"Take off your dress."

Eve turned to face him, his dark gaze dancing in the light of the moon. She was ready to play, she had been a good kitty long enough. Slowly, she lowered her dress, the fabric clinging to her breasts. She was wearing only a delicate white thong, her sex already soaking the little piece of fabric.

Cyrus never took his eyes off her, his gaze roaming her body, no doubt driving him to the brink of madness.

"You forgot something."

Eve smiled. "Take it off yourself."

She had ignited the flames and could no longer extinguish them. Cyrus inched dangerously close, dropping to his knees. Even at this height, he stood taller than her navel. Gently, he gripped the thong at its centre, right where the fabric was damp, lifting it ever so slightly to reveal Eve's bare lips. Holding her breath, she realised that even for the simplest of instructions, he did as he pleased. Cyrus's free hand slid up her ankle, caressing her all the way up her leg to her eager sex.

Eve held her breath as the giant's hand finally found her swollen lips and her awaiting clit, ready to be played with. His fingers began an expert back and forth motion on her clit, eliciting moans of pleasure. Cyrus, still clutching the thong with one hand, bent his face to explore the depths of her intimacy with his tongue. Eve stretched out, her legs weakening beneath her as she grabbed his head, subtly guiding his movements. His tongue like a ballet.

Cyrus paused, his eyes fixated on her, before reaching down to retrieve the thong from her feet. With a swift motion, he tucked it into the back pocket of his pants, much to Eve's disapproval. "A memento."

"Pervert," she muttered under her breath.

He rose to his feet and grabbed her under her buttocks, guiding her to the windowsill. Maintaining intense eye contact, Cyrus fully dedicated himself to her. One hand continued its sensual dance on her clit, the other teasingly exploring her entrance. Slowly and steadily, he inserted a finger, giving Eve time to fully savour the sensation and prepare for more. Her moans and gasps filled the air, and any doubts she had about her decision vanished. Cyrus was fulfilling every promise he had made.

Eve arched her back slightly as Cyrus introduced a second finger, he really had huge fingers, and Eve had not had sex in a long time. Her body quickly got used to the new presence and she had to suppress her loud moans, trying to maintain some semblance of restraint. With two fingers plunging inside her, growing more forceful with each movement, and a hand expertly pleasuring her clit, her climax was approaching rapidly.

"Cyrus, wait... I'm about to come."

"Mmmm hmmm."

"... and you still have your pants on."

Cyrus leaned in, capturing her lips in a passionate kiss, never ceasing the delightful motion of his fingers.

"You'll return the favour later I'm sure," he murmured. "After all, we wouldn't want to get into any trouble."

Eve looked up at the night sky, ready to negotiate when the intensifying rhythm of his fingers left her unable to form coherent thoughts. She gripped her lover's arms so tightly she thought she might hurt him, but the familiar feeling of the wave building inside her overtook her, ready to crash through her entire being.

A gasp escaped her mouth at the third finger inside her tight pussy and she grabbed Cyrus by his neck, holding herself steady while he pushed his fingers forcefully inside her.

"Cyrus..." she moaned, but she was silenced by his lips on her lips, his tongue forcing its way to play with hers. Fingers pumped in and out, twisting while his thumb played with her sensitive nub. Encircling her arms around his shoulders, she deepened their kiss, fully opening herself to him, he sure knew how to kiss, and there was nothing better than a great kisser. Eve moaned her pleasure and pain as Cyrus added a fourth finger.

"Cy..."

"Shhhh. You can take it my Goddess, if your beautiful little pussy can't handle my hand, you are never going to be able to take my dick."

A strong thrust of his hand took her by surprise, eliciting a scream, her nails digging into his shirt and skin. She could no longer hold her loud moans, as she took him fully.

Releasing her mouth, he watched her with such intensity Eve thought she would come just by the strength of his look on her. Taking her arms from his neck, she gripped the window's edge ready to be fucked. She moved her pussy away from him, and while she readjusted herself on the window, she enjoyed watching him licking his fingers, shining from her juice all over them.

Her ass now stabilised, with her back against the cold window, she slowly raised her legs, opening them holding them knee heigh, giving Cyrus a full view of her soaked sex, and full access. Hoping it was driving him just as crazy as she was.

"Fuck me Cyrus."

Unzipping his pants in a swift move, he took out his dick, which was, as promised, huge. Eve gasped as he entered her, in one slow, way too slow, thrust, his left hand holding her by the back of her neck while his right was set on her lower back, assuring her balance. Their eyes locked as he fucked her gently, giving Eve plenty of time to get used to his size, their breath mixing, their lips together, tongues playing passionately with each other.

It was difficult for Eve to hold back her moans, she could feel every inch of Cyrus taking her, and she had never been stretched so much before. *Fuck I missed this.*

"Move me out of the window," she ordered, her poor butt cramping.

He chuckled lifting her. "This wasn't the comfiest position you could have chosen for our first time." Cyrus started walking, still inside her, lifting her up as if she weighed nothing.

"Well what position do you want then, Mr-Smart-Ass?" she barely managed to mutter, moving up and down his cock, his hands cupping her ass cheeks as if they were made for this. *They probably were.* Cyrus took her off his dick, to a grumpy groan as he sat, more like fell on a couch sitting. Hand stroking his dick, gesturing to Eve to come closer, with the naughtiest look she had ever seen on a man before.

"Get to work babe."

With a light laugh Eve went to him excited and jumping around as if it was Christmas and she could finally open her gift. Ready to sit on his lap, one leg on each side, her hands on his shoulders, she lowered herself, taking him slow and deep, holding her breath when the stretch was too much for her, then pushing again, before taking him to the hilt, her head back in ecstasy. She wouldn't be able to walk straight tomorrow, that's for sure.

Cyrus's palms stroked her hips before fully grabbing what he could, moving her up and down his length, to a slow pace, until she placed her hands on his and gave a faster, deeper rhythm.

"Shhhh slowly baby," he muttered, "we don't want to damage that nice little pussy of yours, I am not done with it yet"

"Good," she whispered. "Because I am not done with your giant dick either"

Cyrus laughed again, with his boisterous sound it would be a miracle if nobody heard them.

I just wanted an empty quiet place to get away for a wank. All those tits in all those tight dresses were giving me the hots, and her. *Oh my God, her.* Her dress was the sluttiest dress she had ever worn, and she was the Queen of Sluts.

And there she was, the Queen of Sluts being fucked by the asshole King himself. I watched her, watched her beg to be fucked by him. She didn't even get on her knees for him, what kind of slut forgets that?

HE was not going to like that. HE will lose it when I tell him what I saw, he hated Cyrus maybe even more than me.

Watching her getting licked killed my boner, no thank you, I didn't like that. HE promised me I could fuck her when we finally caught her, but she was a tough one to get. Our time will come, HE was too smart to let the little bitch get away. Tonight will be someone's else turn, like last time.

I had to wait for them to finish before finally leaving the damn library. Pushing the door slowly, I tilted my head, making sure nobody would see me leave the room after them. Other guests must smell the cum all over her slit, right? Is everyone fucking blind?

My steps are angry and fast, this fucking tuxedo way too tight on my neck, I just want to take this tie out. I hate ties, unless I use them to strap a bitch to a chair and rip her tits out.

The voice of an angel came behind. "Are you ok Sir?"

I turned quickly, sweating in my costume, seeing a genuinely worried face of a cute waitress. In the usual black and white outfit for these parties, her tits were so big they begged for me to slash her buttoned shirt.

Women are never nice with me. I know I am ugly. Sometimes they pity me, which pisses me off. This one is just like all the others, but she is prettier, her hair tight in a bun, a wonderful brunette colour in there. *Maybe she'll do?* If I come back to HIM empty handed, he will yell at me like HE always does.

Putting my nicest smile on, I leaned in a little closer. "What time do you finish beautiful?"

She scoffed. They always do. Her eyes freeze, she is entering her *"another ugly asshole"* mode.

"I have a boyfriend" she muttered, walking past me, heading back to the ballroom, her ass swaying left to right taunting me.

Slut. She'll do.

Chapter 14

Eve

The strident alarm of Eve's phone woke her up, which was unusual as her internal clock always woke her up before that awful sound. Eve growled as she tried to reach the damn machine on her bedside table, feeling the wood of the furniture blindly deciding not to open her eyes until she reached her phone. A sigh escaped her when she finally turned the thing off.

Note to self, pick another fucking alarm. Why am I so tired?

Cyrus Fucking McRory.

The man had destroyed her, mostly her pussy, in a good way. They had managed to escape the Gala as discreetly as they could and came back to her place for an insane night of fucking. And an insane Sunday of fucking. It was a lot of fucking for one pussy, and she sure was feeling the effects now.

Eve stretched her back, her favourite cat stretch, yelping in pain. This damn guy broke her, she had to kick him out of her flat last evening, unable to take one more inch of his cock. She grunted sitting as slow as she could on her bed, enjoying the quietness of her apartment. *I'm in trouble...*

She was pretty sure a few people spotted them leaving the Gala, and stupidly she had brought a dangerous man to her killer den. *I am dumb.*

"Oh well." What was done was done. She jumped to her feet, immediately regretting the decision at the ache of her limbs, but eventually she took a quick shower before getting ready for work.

Eve knew something was wrong as soon as she stepped into the station. Taking a deep breath, she advanced towards the stairs leading to her office, Erik was whispering to Andy in front of the anti-psycho room, the rest buzzing behind the closed door.

Her heart accelerated while she tried to climb the stairs steadily, a little bit of guilt was gnawing her after her debauching time with Cyrus. *The police party for fuck's sake.* She could still feel the warmth of Cyrus's hands on her, especially on her lower parts, the man sure knew how to find his way on a woman's body. Her cheeks were burning and red when she finally reached her boss and Andy.

Andy scoffed. "Girl you need to work out a bit harder if ten stairs make you breathless."

Eve chuckled, burning even more. "Yeah, working out sounds good." She looked around feigning ignorance. "What's happening?".

The dark shadow that appeared on both faces screamed it. Her heart accelerated. *The psycho did it again.* He loved to kill even more than she did, which was already quite an unbelievable truth. She sighed before they could say anything. "Do you need me in the meeting?"

Erik nodded, a strange glint in his eyes while he looked at her, before inviting her to follow them into the special anti-psycho office. Eve quickly ran to her desk first to drop her jacket, making sure to leave her phone. She refused to handle sexting with Cyrus right now when the next hour or so was going to be a presentation of dreaded pictures.

An hour later Eve was finally out of the room, nausea threatening her stomach. This body was worse than the last one, even worse than the one before that. This time the killer seemed to have unleashed all his anger on the poor woman, her body was nothing like it should be. She had been raped, multiple times, in every way possible, including with sharp objects. Her breasts had been sliced up and down, reducing what used to be the apogee of her femininity to a shredded flesh cluster. The pain she must have gone through was gut wrenching to imagine, and Eve could feel the tears coming every time she thought about it.

The psycho was losing his mind, he was becoming crazy — well, crazier — and she didn't need to be a profiler to know he was furious. She sure hoped Ian, who was supposed to arrive soon, was not going to ask that the team make the killer angrier. Something they did multiple times, over and over again, in her favourite thrillers.

She sighed, stretching her back, a well-deserved cup of coffee in her hand and tensed up at the voice behind her.

"Tough weekend?"

Eve scoffed and turned on her heels, to see Ian, his long auburn hair tidy in a neat bun, a light of mischief in his beautiful blue eyes. His grey pants and sky-blue shirt making him look, for once, professional. He sure was a handsome man as well. *No wonder Zorfield is all over him.* She liked him, in the middle of all her crazy banging with Cyrus, they had managed to have actual conversations, and Cyrus obviously admired his best friend.

"Yeah tough, had to stay in bed all week..."

Erik arrived in the break room, interrupting her.

"...was so siiick," she finished, accompanying her last words with an uncomfortable chuckle.

Erik glanced at her, and Eve swore he had a knowing gleam in his eyes, the same she spotted earlier. *Could he know?* Or was she just imagining it, her guilt taking over any common sense? She immediately stopped breathing and took a big chug of her drink, promising herself to be more careful in the future.

Busy with her thoughts, she hadn't been listening to the exchange between the two men which appeared quite cordial, before Erik guiding Ian towards the anti-psycho room quickly turned to Eve and asked her to join as well. Eve held back a sigh, she really would have preferred not to look at the hideous pictures again. She was not that sensitive usually, but it hurt her in a different way when she was looking at the bodies of those poor women, increasing her rage, little by little.

She climbed the stairs quickly, not wanting to have the team wait for her, and arrived right on time to see Bonnie welcome Ian, her usual smile on her lips, while Andy sat on his desk, crossed arms with a pouting face that did not fit him at all. Eve went to him anyway, sitting by his side giving him a light elbow, whispering, "hey stop pouting, we need him, I heard he's good."

Andy grumbled which made her snicker, but immediately stopped when she felt Erik's eyes on her.

Angry. He was angry. Eve straightened on the desk before jumping off it, heading for her favourite corner, her heart racing, a lump forming in her stomach. Erik had NEVER been angry at her, but she knew she was right, he was pissed off at her, meaning he had to know about her adventure with Cyrus.

Deciding to forget about it for the moment, after all what you don't think about can't hurt you, right? She focused on the psychopath. If Erik knew something he would talk to her about it. Until then, she would act as innocent as a virgin. Kind of. She sat in her corner, biting her lips, not sure she was ready for another go at the pictures; but she was curious to know what Ian thought about the increased violence. She had the impression that Andy and Bonnie weren't even sure where to start, thankfully Ian took the lead.

"Forget about the older victims, I want to see the new one first, we need to focus on her for now." Ian rolled up his sleeves, showing off muscular but thin forearms.

Eve couldn't stop a shiver spotting the various lines, so parallel they looked like a work of art, the pink colours contrasting with his snow-white skin.

Ian observed every picture of the new body, spending so long on each one that she wondered how he could not have nightmares. He furrowed his brows, observing a picture of her face, a bloody, bruised, mush of a face, as if trying to place a name on the woman. "Where was she found?"

"Still the same," Andy retorted with a smirk. At Ian's interrogative look he pursued. "In your friend's territory."

Ian responded with a derisive scoff.

"I will keep an open mind on this profile, as I promised Erik." He turned to the Commander. "But I don't need to be friends with Cyrus to tell you right now he has no connection to this case. Bodies dropping in his neighbourhood means very little."

Andy sighed, rolling his eyes. "Well one could hope, right?"

"What about the first victim?" Ian asked. "Where was she found? And what did her body look like after... this..."

Andy pushed another stack of pictures and the accompanying file towards Ian, July's murder.

As Ian reached for the documents, he turned to Bonnie, who appeared tense in her chair. "Something wrong Bonnie?"

The beautiful woman hesitated a minute. "I don't think Roisin was the first victim, I think there is another one, one that has been... erm.... overlooked."

Eve raised her head, not surprised Bonnie might have picked up something the others had missed. She was the best. With Andy, yes, but Andy was more efficient in a brutish way.

Ian grabbed the thin file Bonnie handed him.

"We have no concrete proof whatsoever that the prostitute was indeed the first victim," Erik said. "She was not tortured the same way, she was vulgar while the others all have some sort of... class..." Erik cleared his throat. "And well, hard to know if she was raped or if it's simply from work."

At Ian's blank look, Erik continued, "This is mostly likely a day at work gone bad, we should focus on the other ones."

"I disagree, Erik, it won't add much work for me to go through it. First victims often provide insight into the mind of the serial killer, they are their first after all. She's important to him, not to mention he could have made mistakes then."

Bonnie flashed a grateful smile to the redhead, and Eve thought she spotted some kind of recognition in Andy as well.

"As you wish, you are the expert after all." Erik sighed, glancing at his watch. "I am sorry Ian, I have a meeting that I can't escape, but Eve will stay and take notes so I can review them later."

Ian nodded with a smile, while Eve for the first time felt relieved Erik was leaving the room. The notion that he might not want to solve the murders briefly crossed her mind.

After all it was of common knowledge that bribes and politics were ruling the police world, and perhaps Cragnum had finally managed to get a hold in her friend. But worrying for her old friend that he could be in any kind of trouble, had to wait, and she quickly came back to the conversation, feeling if she messed up her report, she would hear about it.

Chapter 15

Eve

The long-awaited Opera night had arrived, and Eve was relieved to escape the relentless discussions surrounding the recent murders. Even for her, the situation was beginning to weigh heavily on her shoulders. Besides, she had been so busy at work lately she didn't have time to meet up with Cyrus despite their constant sexts and their OMG-what-would-my-mum-say videos. They were also calling each other every night, which at first she found weird, but quickly started waiting with impatience for the daily call, enjoying their talks.

More than often their talks were derivative on the naughty side, and she was now so horny she was ready to beg him for his dick to be inside her again. And Cyrus gladly sending a close up of his dick, hard and leaking pre-cum, was not helping. Eve had stopped counting the number of times she had to use her favourite toy to relieve herself, wishing it was Cyrus instead.

She cast a questioning look toward the door at the sound of the doorbell, her body responding with a shiver, sensing his presence. She glanced quickly at her reflection in the full-length mirror by her apartment's entrance. A towel. That was all. As always, Cyrus had arrived early, and she couldn't help but wonder if he did it intentionally to catch her unprepared. With a wry smile, she opened the door, facing the stunning man before her. Cyrus remained still, leaning casually against the door frame, his eyes unmistakably appreciating Eve's unconventional attire.

"You're early," she accused.

"I was in the neighbourhood. Thought it wouldn't be a problem to be early."

Liar. His knowing smirk said he knew she knew he was lying. She welcomed him inside, fully aware he would simply do as he pleased anyway, and she needed a bit more time to prepare. After all, it wasn't every day she received an invitation to the Opera.

Especially not when she had intended to wear her new emerald-green velvet strapless dress, which hugged her figure perfectly. She bought it with the slight hope it would entice Cyrus to go down on her again, and who knows, maybe even more.

Cyrus entered and a warm presence brushed against his legs. Lowering his head, he looked at the black kitten rubbing against him.

"It's Neko. My cat." Eve smiled. "He was hiding the last time you came."

"And today he purrs and cuddles me, just like his mistress, such a good kitty. Enchanted Neko." Cyrus smiled, his fingers tenderly caressing the kitten's ears.

Eve gave Cyrus the sternest look she could, but her resistance crumbled when he winked at her. She playfully rolled her eyes, walking to her room. "Sooo... I'm going to get dressed now, before you get any weird ideas involving that humongous dick of yours."

"Too late," the giant said, his intense ocean blue eyes locked on her body. "And if I remember right, you enjoyed my 'humongous' dick so much last time you were climbing me like a tree."

Eve scoffed, ready to answer something for sure witty to that last comment, but she inadvertently dropped her gaze, intending to scold Neko for his apparent betrayal, and couldn't help but notice that Cyrus appeared rather tight in his trousers.

"Fuck it!" Eve sighed. She let the towel slip from her grasp, allowing it to fall to the ground. Cyrus grunted as his gaze met her body.

"Eve... Are you aware that you are getting into trouble... again?"

"Oopsie." She shrugged, advancing towards him, sticking her body against him, moving naturally to mould his shape until she could finally feel his erection against her. *This man is way too tall.* She raised her hands, catching his strong face between them, bringing him down for a kiss.

Immediately he grabbed her by the hips, trying to get her even closer. He lowered his gigantic hands to her buttocks, lifting her up as if she was as light as a feather, while she surrounded his hips with her naked legs pressing against him. He advanced towards the couch and threw Eve on it and she made a disappointed pout. "I was hoping for a ride to the bedroom." Cyrus laughed, pushing her onto the couch, pulling her lower body towards the edge of it, getting on his knees.

Cyrus

"You are gonna make us late, Little One," Cyrus grumbled, before his tongue hit her clit, there was no need for more foreplay than this. Crystalline laughter left Eve, right before transforming into moaning. God he loved how loud she was, he would never get enough of her little squeals.

Slowly he moved his hands, pushing on Eve's thighs to have her perfectly opened for him, admiring her tender pussy, fully bare, already glistening of her own juice. Eve was so easy to turn on. He smirked, remembering their first time, and how well she took most of his hand, he wondered if he should give the full fist a go tonight, Eve seemed even more excited than usual.

His tongue worked up and down her little nub, alternating hard and soft licks, following Eve's moans to answer her desires. He would never get enough of her taste either. He never understood why men were not fond of it, there was nothing better than being covered by a woman's pleasure. His tongue played hard on her cunt, played inside her, drinking her full juice, while his thumb tortured her sensitive clit, until he finally added a finger. A gasp had him lifting his head to meet Eve's eyes, her beautiful hazel eyes were filled with more lust than he had witnessed in his life.

"I want more, Cyrus," she begged, her lips wet and half open in a lustful sound.

Cyrus snickered. "Remember how you jumped at the sensation of four fingers fucking you last time?" He added his middle finger not stopping his light thrust, getting as deep as he could, twisting.

"Humhum." Eve closed her eyes.

"I think tonight you can have more my Goddess..."

Eve opened her eyes, brows furrowed. "More than your, once again, humongous dick? I highly doubt that, I could barely walk after that, some of us have to work you know."

A deep laughter came with a third finger, her body tightening around it, her breath scattered over the new invasion. A lick of her clit accompanied his new sneaky fourth finger.

At Eve's moans, he slowed down a bit, examining her face, distorted between pleasure and pain, tears coming to her eyes. This would have been the best thing he'd ever seen until she took the next step, holding her own legs, spreading as much as she could, knees as high as her breast.

"Ask me."

"Please... Cyrus..." Eve gasped, tensing when Cyrus took out his fingers, and sucked on his thumb.

"Please what?" he asked, positioning his fist at the entrance of her pussy, more drenched than he had ever seen another woman before. He started inserting his fist, feeling her body stretch under his closed hands.

Eve

"Fist me." Eve had never felt so naughty before, so horny for a man. And she had never wanted to be fisted before, what a funny idea it was, especially with a dick as perfect as Cyrus's.

"Make me yours" she begged, letting go of a leg to play with her clit, letting out a deep growl when she felt Cyrus's entire hand penetrate her. The pain was there, pulling, stretching her cunt, but it brought a different kind of pleasure, one that screams to you that you are finally being filled, as you should.

Her hand accelerated, torturing her clit with precision, eyes locked on Cyrus's ocean eyes, devouring her with his burning look. Her new scream had him growling as if he was some kind of wild beast.

"You're driving me insane my Goddess, I want to fuck you so hard I don't even know where to start." He pulled back his fist, triggering little squeals.

With a grunt he grabbed her behind her neck, forcing her to stand on wobbly legs, her lips half-opened, cheeks red, drops of sweat following the curve of her breast. He brought her face close to his.

"I can't believe how you taking me, you are such a fucking good girl."

"I'm not," a raspy voice answered.

"No?" Cyrus chuckled, strengthening his grip on her.

"What are you gonna do about it?" Eve placed her hand on his dick, squeezing lightly.

Cyrus chuckled pushing his front a bit more into Eve's hand.

"I think we're going to be late to the Opera if we don't stop now."

Chapter 16

Eve

Thirty minutes later they were finally pulling up to the Opera after a drive filled with sexual tension that would make the Marquis de Sade blush. Eve was still on fire, her juices leaking onto her thighs, her poor pussy screaming for help after Cyrus's fist invasion, even though it had been way too short.

She was at least glad to see she wasn't the only one in this poor situation, Cyrus never came, and she honestly wondered how he was holding up with such blue balls. He had not let her touch him, invoking the "late arrival to the Opera" reason which made Eve more than frustrated, she really didn't care about the Opera anymore.

Who cared about sad, singing people when she could sing Cyrus's name all night? She had come harder than ever with him fisting her, and she wouldn't be surprised if her neighbours heard her.

Cyrus veered toward an underground parking area instead of stopping where the other guests were disembarking. Intrigued, she cast a curious glance his way.

"I have a private spot," he said holding up a key.

"At the Opera?" Eve asked with a hint of amusement, almost on the verge of laughter.

"Ian adores the Opera. Tries to bring us here as often as possible. So, I figured it would be more convenient, and financially sensible, to secure a parking space."

Eve held back a laugh while Cyrus parked the car. Things were just so... natural with him, so easy.

Once parked in an elegant manoeuvre that she would never been able to do despite having been driving for 10 years, she playfully reached over and grabbed his thigh, holding him back from exiting the car. He looked at her, a snarky smile on his lips, his brows up in the air with this look of a lost puppy he was handling so well.

"Don't think you're going to get away with it," she warned with a mischievous grin.

Cyrus burst into laughter and leaned in for a kiss, but Eve countered placing a finger against his chest, firmly keeping him in his seat. He scoffed, surrendering to Eve's playful dominance, letting out a low growl as her hand ventured lower, tracing the contours of his swelling trousers.

Cyrus closed his eyes, his breathing accelerating as Eve gently opened his fly. Keeping her eyes on Cyrus's, she caught his huge dick, positioning herself better on her seat.

Spreading his pre-cum with her thumb on the tip, she started expertly moving back and forth, taking her time, enjoying his length. Apparently there was such a thing as a perfect cock. He was so large she couldn't close her hand. Thoughts of his dick inside of her again had the moisture in her thong intensifying.

Cyrus moaned loudly when she finally leaned over, playing with her tongue, licking the tip in a circle, before tasting him.

Cyrus

Cyrus violently grabbed her head, forcing his erected dick into Eve's mouth, throbbing under the tightness of her jaw, and to his intense satisfaction she didn't seem to mind a bit. He couldn't stop himself, observing her smooth hair flying around as she moved up and down, taking him almost in his entirety. He could hear her struggle when he pushed on her head a bit harder, wanting her to take him to his base.

Grabbing her hair, he pulled her head up to face him, her face bright red had what looked like pre-cum around her mouth. Her breath was scattered and for once, he felt as if he had some power over her. This excited him more than anything before. Holding her hair with one hand, catching her jaw with the other, he brought her in for a kiss.

"You can do better than that, my Goddess. Take all of me, make this sweet little mouth stretch and make me come. I want your mouth to feel like I am home."

He twisted the long mass of gorgeous brunette hair, holding it around his wrist and hand. Eve's head fell back with the pull, her chest moving fast, her breast almost out of their velvet prison, her neck entirely offered.

"Make me take you," she whispered in a raspy voice.

Eve

She was plunged back on his dick, going deeper and deeper, losing her breath on the size of him. His hand was still holding her hair in a ferocious hold, and she was not surprised when he started pushing her back and forth, accompanying her movements until she found her rhythm.

With satisfaction she finally managed to fit him in her mouth, his tip reaching her throat, quickening her pace on the perfect dick. Only to be pulled away in a forceful movement. This man was NOT scared of teeth.

"What again Master?" she joked. "Not deep enough?"

Cyrus laughed. "I like that. You should call me that way more often."

Eve scoffed. "You wish."

"Well I don't think you're done darling, my dick still wants to come inside this sweet good girl mouth of yours."

He let go of her hair to adjust himself, getting his pants lower on his legs, leaving Eve free. Opening the car door quickly, she jumped out, giggling.

When she bent down to look at the man, pants on his ankles, a puzzled look on his face she could not stop the heartfelt laugh.

"Now we can go," she said, adjusting her strapless dress, which had somewhat revealed bits of her chest in the heat of the moment.

"Fucking hell Eve, get back here." Cyrus tried to catch her, but she was already too far for his reach, sticking her tongue out at him.

The man grunted, promptly pulled his pants up and got out of the car. Before she had time to flee further, he grabbed her swinging her against him, making sure she could feel his hard dick. Eve was breathless.

"Don't think you're going to get away with this." He released her in a fast move, and with both hands grabbed the top of her dress, lowering her bustier, revealing her two erect nipples. He caught them between his fingers and pinched firmly, twisting them, drawing a little cry of pain from Eve.

"Cyrus..." she tried in a weak voice as the pressure on her breasts grew stronger, but she fell silent when his tongue went in her mouth. He grabbed her hips, turning her against the bonnet of the car.

"You wouldn't dare??" Eve scorned, outraged.

"Let me see..."

Eve gasped, his enormous fingers slipping into her slit, teasing her, moving up and down along the wetness, tickling her clit. She knew she was drenched of her own juice, but now Cyrus knew it too.

"That's what I thought," Cyrus whispered, bending over her. "I'm so glad you like it a bit rough." He started back and forth with his fingers, playing her clit with his left hand. "Now the question is, how rough can you take my Goddess?"

Eve moaned, she thought she wouldn't be able to take another inch tonight, but her body was proving her wrong. She would totally take his dick up to the hilt right now, who cared about being able to walk the following day. Her sex was pulsating with desire, and she was so wet she could barely feel his fingers.

Cyrus moved her long legs, opening them wide, pulling her dress up, revealing Eve's butt, beautifully wrapped in a black lingerie thong.

"Hmmmm... what am I gonna do with that perfection of an ass?" Cyrus teased. "Spread those cheeks darling, show me this tight hole of yours."

Eve gasped, he was SO naughty, and she sure hoped fisting her ass wouldn't come to his mind. But her excitement took over, and slowly she spread her cheeks, the thong getting stuck in the middle. A groan answered the gesture, and she felt the giant's hands pulling her ass cheeks apart, thumbs lightly stroking her burning skin, before something wet touched her butthole. Eve's moans started to resonate in the empty parking garage, she was officially a big fan of Cyrus's tongue, and she would not mind him having some ass-play right now.

She managed to keep her cheeks apart, giving a clear path for the hungry mouth, feeling the slick tongue piercing her ass, tasting her as much as it could, knowing no limits. The lovely play stopped when Cyrus brought his face close to Eve's, nibbling at her ear, pushing his hips against her ass.

"So...what is it gonna be my Goddess?" He didn't stop his slight hip movement, and Eve tightened at the intrusion of a finger in her ass. A huge finger. Her moans grew louder while she adjusted herself on the car, her hand moving to her clit.

"You would be open to it, would you?" Cyrus whispered, his voice darkened by desire. "You want me to fuck this tight little hole of yours? Take you like the good girl you are?"

Louder moans came at his words, she would reach her climax soon.

"Tell me you're mine, Genevieve."

"I am yours, now fuck me, wherever you want." Eve circled her nub faster.

Without hesitation, he thrust inside her pussy, and after she unclenched his cock, he came out entirely, just to thrust in her again. And again.

"I am keeping your ass for later."

Cyrus and his passionate thrusts were driving her crazy, and she couldn't stop howling her pleasure, taking him entirely. Cyrus growled grabbing her arms, moving them behind her back, keeping her face against his car. Accelerating the pace, fast and hard, in an attempt to go even deeper. He gave a few hard thrusts and Eve's walls tighten even more, her hands trying to reach his wrists in desperate moves. He let go of his hold on her head to slap her ass, a nice, light stroke at first, but after Eve's moans he hit harder.

It didn't take long before Eve howled her orgasm and completely surrendered to Cyrus for the second time that evening. Reaching the intense wave at the same time, Eve had not felt so strong in years, she could not help but let out a satisfied sigh. The lovers collapsed against the hood, breathing heavy and fast.

Moments later Cyrus withdrew, and Eve let out a growl standing up, laying her head against his chest, feeling his rapid breath raising his strong body up and down.

"What if we postponed the Opera to next time?" Cyrus proposed with a naughty smile.

Eve chuckled, nodding, trying to correct her dress, which was a little sticky.

They got back in the car, and Cyrus reached for his phone, dialling Zorfield. Eve stared at him wide-eyed, he wouldn't dare call his friend to tell him the latest gossips of her naked ass on the car?

"Hey," Zorfield answered.

"Zorf. Opera, cameras, especially the one in the parking garage... erase everything."

Eve sighed, of course, the McRory son had access to and controlled everything. Though she was certainly not going to complain about it this time.

"Okay."

Cyrus hung up and started the engine.

"And what if he decides to watch our little video?" Eve asked with a puzzled raised eyebrow.

Cyrus chuckled. "It's quite possible, but you have nothing to fear from him. Worst case, he'll make a snarly comment, best, he'll try to convince Ian to do the same."

They finally left the parking garge, heading towards the boulevard. Eve sensed Cyrus hesitated for a moment and looked at him inquisitively.

"How about going to my place instead? I have a bigger bed, and we can have breakfast in bed." He did complain about the size of her bed the other night, she thought it was more than an acceptable size, but the giant disagreed.

"You had me at breakfast in bed." Eve smiled. "But I'd like to swing by my place to grab some extra clothes."

"Sure thing."

Cyrus parked at the bottom of Eve's building and as she reached for the door handle, he gently held her by the arm, pulling her closer, stealing a sudden, impulsive kiss. Eve laughed and pulled away.

"Give me 5 minutes. I just need to grab a few things and change my dress, that YOU destroyed."

Nodding, Cyrus turned off the engine.

Eve entered her building, cheeks flushed, her sex on fire. She had lost all sense of responsibility. Which didn't make her very proud. But he was driving her crazy.

Ascending two steps at a time, she could feel the burn of Cyrus's hands on her poor butt, and noticed that the automatic lights weren't working, casting the corridor into darkness. Eve hoped it was just temporary, she really could not remember where the hell she placed her flashlight. She slowed down and sighed, trying to find the flashlight-making-thing on her phone, thank technology.

Finally reaching her floor, she found it dimly lit by a few emergency lights. The dark corridor stretched before her eyes, and she had a moment of faint panic, a very old fear waking up. She would feel much better if she had one of her knives with her.

Her keys jingled as she took them out of her tiny purse, and after a few seconds of a feverish keyhole search, she finally opened the door. As soon as she set a foot in her apartment, she felt something was wrong. Her phone rang startling her like a little girl.

Seeing Ian's name added to her already raging anxiety. She answered, whispering a faint "Allo."

"Eve??" Ian's voice sounded panicked. "Where are you? Are you with Cyrus?"

"No... no I'm at home, Cyrus is..." A rustling noise in the living room had her heart racing. A massive shadow loomed over her, and before she knew it, a strong arm grabbed her from the front, effortlessly lifting her off her feet. Her phone slipped from her hand, as Ian called her name through the line.

Her assailant pushed on her ribs, and she began to panic. She knew how to fight but she also knew that confronted with too much physical strength she would be useless without a weapon. Her vulnerability apparent when he threw her against the wall, her head banging violently. Dazed, her survival instinct kicked in and she tried in vain to kick or grab, even bite the man's face, but he escaped all her attempts at cannibalism.

As her consciousness slipped away, she hoped Ian would call Cyrus in time. *Let the big guys fight!* She fell into the darkness, warm blood running down the back of her head.

124

Chapter 17

The little bitch crumpled to the floor like a doll, her body limp, her breathing shallow. Satisfaction pulses through me, thrumming in my chest. I finally did it. I finally got her. She's mine now, she's ours, and I can touch her... I don't think I hurt her head too hard, but bending over to touch her gorgeous hair my hand feels sticky. But she's breathing, so it should be fine.

My breathing is rapid, I can't help myself at the view of her tits barely holding in her dress. My fingers graze her cheek, and the softness of her skin makes me shudder. A strange sound comes out of my throat, like a whine. SO SOFT. She fought like a tiger, we knew we would have to use the surprise to our advantage, she's not like the others. And we are definitely not going to treat her like the others.

Reaching to my pants, I grab my hardened dick through the fabric, wincing under my own touch. That's when I hear it. The footsteps. Loud, frantic, heavy. Climbing the wooden stairs of the building.

"Fuck!"

I jump to my feet, fear clawing at my throat. It's him. It has to be him. Cyrus. He's coming for her, this guy has all the patience of a toddler seeking chocolate. We said we wanted him dead, but not when I'm alone, I don't stand a chance. My hands tremble as I pull her up, she's heavier than I thought. Struggling to lift her, feeling her dead weight on my shoulder, her head rolls at an awkward angle, her hair tickling me. Blood drips from her wound and I can barely hold her steady as I rush toward the door. Stepping in the dark corridor I slam the door shut behind me, hearing the automatic lock. *One of those.* I sure hope it will keep Cyrus busy a while, thinking she's still inside, but she won't be.

I run, or at least try, and dart around the corner, my breath ragged and uneven. The footsteps behind me enter the long corridor. Cyrus is getting closer. I push myself harder, faster, Eve's weight dragging me down, I can't help but let a whine escape at the thought of losing her so close to our goal. The back stairs, all dark and metallic, brighten as the automatic light turns on. My heart speeds up, but I can't stop now. Grabbing the ramp with one hand, I start climbing down the tight steps, there's no point trying to be discreet now, I can hear him. He's reached the door. One bump. Two bumps, and I know the freaking door is down, it didn't hold him anywhere near long enough. His footsteps move towards me.

Panic surges. I have to move faster, but my legs are starting to give up, and under the pressure I can feel a bit of pee running along my legs. I barely catch myself before my ankle rolls, missing a step. I hear the pounding from above, and my blood runs cold. He's right there, almost on me.

And then — I drop her. The weight is too much. The terror paralyses me. She falls to the ground between two floors with a sickening thud. And I run.

Reaching the ground floor, I hear the steps above me slow, his raging voice calling Eve's name, with bliss I open the door and run in the night towards the vehicle waiting for me. I can already hear the punishment. HE'll make me pay for this.

Chapter 18

Eve

Eve awoke to a throbbing pain in her skull and anxious faces surrounding her. Her heart skipped a beat when her damaged brain recognised police uniforms, her first instinct screaming at her this was it, everyone knew about her night hobby - *oh hey there guilt*.

A blond lady with a paramedic uniform approached her, a blood pressure monitor in hand. An awkward smile on her lips, she silently surrounded Eve's biceps with the cold plastic.

Once done Eve attempted to stand, her vision still a bit blurry, her headache getting worse, she would rather lie down but the feeling of those unfriendly glances upon her was not promoting relaxation right now. She gave up standing when her head spun, deciding the couch would do just fine, who cares about unfriendly watchers? She muttered something noticing the state of her dress, barely holding her breasts in place, stained by her passionate sex session with Cyrus. *Fuck.*

She adjusted the fabric as best as she could, and sat down. That's when she finally understood the reason for the disturbing silence and the mean looks. Her eyes met Cyrus, sitting on her sofa, facing her. She was surprised she hadn't noticed him earlier, seeing that the giant was taking all the couch by himself. He had a furious look that she was glad she had never seen directed at her. His eyes darker than ever, his jaw clenched, eyebrows furrowed as if he was thinking way too hard for his brain.

Despite his furious look, she couldn't help but giggle when she spotted the handcuffs around his wrists, not to mention the two young policemen surrounding him, clearly wishing they were somewhere else. Cyrus rolled his eyes at her reaction, and sat back against the couch, indistinct grumbling coming out of his mouth. Despite her headache, Eve couldn't stop the instant fire growing inside her at the view of her lover. The man was sitting legs wide open, typical Alpha, his fancy shirt rolled up to his elbows, showing off muscular forearms. Gosh she loved forearms. The handcuffs were giving her way too many ideas for later.

"Eve," a voice on her side distracted her from the handsome giant. *Oh shit.*

Andy, with Bonnie at his side, didn't look pleased. "We REALLY need you to tell us what happened." They were both standing, arms crossed, faces showing how unimpressed they were with her.

Eve shrugged. "A guy was waiting for me in my apartment, he assaulted me, I fainted and... well... here we are... Did you guys search my apartment?" she asked, worried. Her senses had now returned, and she didn't feel comfortable at the thought of all those policemen and her sexy lover invading her killer den.

"And who assaulted you?" Andy asked.

Eve stared at him with an incredulous look. "Do you mean you haven't caught him yet? Man that's not worth the headache I am getting now. Why did he run away then?"

As far as she could tell, the guy was quite dedicated to getting her, so leaving her behind? Really?

"It's up to you to tell me," Andy said nodding in Cyrus direction, who looked at Eve with an air far too naughty for her taste, giving her his trademark sexy-eyebrow-raise. Flashbacks of orgasm on the hood of his car assaulted her, but she had the decency to blush. "It... It wasn't Cyrus."

"Hallelujah!" Cyrus shook his handcuffs towards Andy. "Your old hag of a neighbour saw me forcing my way into your apartment and had the GREAT idea to call our friends. Who as usual are showing their skills."

Andy growled in apparent disappointment, motioning for one of the policemen to release Cyrus. Immediately, Cyrus stood and walked towards Eve. He knelt before her, and the police in the room followed suit, which surprised Eve. She widened her eyes and tried to mentally communicate with Cyrus that no, really, this was not the right time for such a display. But he remained silent gazing at her, lifting his hand to tenderly place a strand of hair behind her ear.

Screams came from the front door, and Eve couldn't take the time to appreciate the gesture, which truth be told was quite different to the whole "should I fuck your ass now or later?" stuff he gave her earlier.

Ian and Zorfield busted into her apartment. Ian seemed shaken, while Zorfield was provoking the police attempting to restrain them.

Andy sighed. "Leave them be," he said with a gest of his hand, as if accepting the inevitable that he would not be able to arrest Cyrus today. "Eve, we'll need to take your statement Monday. For tonight, you should stay home and rest. I'll assign two policemen to be on duty here, seeing that your door is down."

Cyrus shot Andy a dark glance but returned lost in his contemplation of Eve while she tried to look at her door.

"Why is my door down?" she yelled.

"I kicked it down to open it," Cyrus mumbled. "I didn't know it was so weak."

Eve glanced at him.

"Really? Weak? You are so paying for it."

Cyrus rolled his eyes but nodded.

Andy snapped his fingers. "Eve. Focus. We suspect it's our lady killer. It's not safe here."

Eve nodded, it seemed obvious to her that it was indeed her freaking nemesis of a killer, looked like he found her before she even had the slightest idea about where to find him. Which truth be told, didn't look good at all.

"And you Cyrus," Andy continued, "we're going to LOVE taking your statement at the station on Monday and figuring out how you ended up in the wrong place, at the wrong time, with the wrong person."

"You mean the right time, in the right place?" Ian interjected. "Cyrus arrived in time to save Eve, don't waste your time with him Andy."

"He still needs to give a statement," Andy replied firmly. His newborn respect for the redhead seemed to have vanished.

"And he'll be there, with his favourite lawyer. Me," Ian said with a smile. *A lawyer?* Was there anything this guy couldn't do?

Andy growled again and beckoned the troops to leave.

Cyrus finally stood up. "Don't bother leaving your guys here. Eve won't be sleeping in her apartment tonight."

Andy turned to him. "Then where does Eve plan to sleep?" Hands on his hips, he gave Eve a look that expressed all of his not-impressed-with-you-right-now feels.

Eve sighed. "Eve is a grown woman who decides where she wants to spend the night, Andy. I'm not going to sleep here. And I don't need the police to watch me."

She would be much safer in Cyrus's arms away from the serial killer.

A few minutes later the horde of police and paramedics finally left, Andy and Bonnie reluctantly walking through the door. Andy turned. "Do I call Erik or do you do it?"

At Eve's cold stare, he left the apartment without further ado. Eve tried to rise from the couch, feeling that all of this would not end well. Cyrus remained silent, standing by the window. Numerous questions swirled in her mind, making her feel a bit queasy.

Ian, who had been sneaking around the flat, to Eve's distress, broke the silence. "He's a policeman." Eve looked at him questioningly. "The killer. I think he's a policeman."

"The fact that they spend their time trying to put your best friend in jail is not proof Ian," Eve said, rubbing her tired eyes.

"Explain it to her." Cyrus crossed his arms.

Ian sighed. "Okay, it's still a theory, but I went back to the start of the crimes and looked at everything."

"Oh right, those files," Cyrus interjected sarcastically. "You know, the ones you secretly gave to my best friend."

Eve shot him an angry look. "You mean the confidential files I entrusted to your best friend, the profiler who's been denied showcasing his talents to the world because of his association with you? There's a psychopathic killer on the loose, Cyrus."

He smirked. "More than one."

"That's not the point here," Ian sighed turning to Cyrus. "Besides, you could have easily found out what I was doing. Erik and Eve were right to request confidentiality towards you, or else my findings would be relentlessly challenged by a bunch of asshole lawyers. Even YOU know that Cyrus."

Cyrus turned, a mischievous grin on his face. "Unless they can't get their hands on the killer. Accidents happen so quickly. No body no crime."

Though Eve agreed with his point, she wasn't going to say it, settling for watching Cyrus and Zorfield give each other a high five. She pouted, the killer was her target, and she wasn't going to let Cyrus steal her prey. *Next time I'll be ready.*

Ian sighed. "The killer started a little haphazardly. Bonnie was right, the prostitute was the first, I'm sure of it. He just had no idea what he liked to do, he might not have planned to kill her at first, he was probably just looking for some hardcore sex, then things went wild."

Ian took a break, Eve knew he was thinking about how exactly "things went wild," and it was not pretty, they both saw the pictures.

"First thing I spotted, which honestly could mean nothing without any other proof, were the physical features of the ladies. He started choosing pretty little Irish girls. Both the prostitute and the July crime are blond, clear eyes, luscious bodies." Ian shook his head. "Not the last three. All September murders are different, it has to mean something. He chooses them thinner, browner, with darker eyes, a more 'warm look.' We have an evolution of the body he is aiming for. Which made me think something changed, something caught his attention." Ian showed pictures of the young women in their lifetime.

A pinch plagued Eve's heart when she saw all the beautiful women who had their lives ahead of them before crossing paths with this guy. Ian was right, he had moved on to a more South-European style. And she thought she knew where he was going with that.

"Are you telling me I'm in his new category?" That was not something she was excited about.

"I think you're the one he wants, but he couldn't have you and had to refer to others to satisfy his urge to hurt and to kill. Hence the violence."

Eve shook her head. "No Ian, it's too crazy and too easy. Just because he chooses long, dark, messy hair, doesn't mean…"

"I looked at the dates Eve, they don't lie…"

He opened the notebook in his hand, showing Eve and his two acolytes who had come closer a diagram.

Cyrus sat next to Eve, more tense than usual, cracking his fingers in an annoying manner.

"Ok. First murder: June 27, the prostitute. Second murder: July 18, one of Cyrus's playthings."

Cyrus coughed and received a dark look from Eve.

"Then the type of prey changes. September 3rd: third murder, more violence compared to the last ones, another of Cyrus's… friend," Ian amended under the frenetic look from Cyrus. "Next one, found on Tuesday September 25th, but everything leads to her kidnapping a few days earlier on the 21st. Couldn't point anything to Cyrus this time, which is good. And the next one, found on Monday the 1st, disappeared on Saturday the 29th, the most violent to this date."

Eve was still waiting to find out how she could have a role to play in all of this, this was exactly the reason why she was leaving the detective part to someone else. *Can we get to the slash-slash-kill-kill part?*

"When did you arrive in Ireland, Eve?"

"Hum… August 31. I started work on the 2nd."

"And where were you on the evening of Friday, September 21st?"

Eve frowned, she certainly didn't remember everything she did, especially since some of her evenings were usually a little special.

Cyrus replied for her, brooding at her side. "You were with me. Our first date"

"Oh right, probably why I'd rather not remember it."

"That's not what you were saying in the lift."

Cyrus swiftly moved out of the way when a pink cushion flew close to his head.

"What about Saturday, September 29th?" Ian interrupted them.

"The Gala!" Eve announced in a victorious voice, happy to be able to re-member something in her life.

"And what did you do at that Gala and during the weekend?" Ian asked, giving her a mischievous look.

Eve blushed, while Cyrus sneered. She elbowed him.

"What's your point?" she asked.

"You were 'busy' the two nights the other two young women were abducted. You were with another man, a man who is certainly hated by the killer too."

Cyrus began to protest, but Eve cut him off. "But why would he be part of the police force? Just because I work there?"

"He must have met you somewhere, and you spend all your time working." *And killing.*

"Just kidding," Ian laughed. "There's also the fact that the victims were all abducted from their flat, with no sign of a break in. You only let people enter if you trust them. And there were no signs of the victims having a power provider or such. But if someone came, a police officer uniform and all, anyone would open the door." Eve had a lot to say about trusting the police but decided it was not the time.

She sighed. "I mean... It could have been anywhere on the street as well. Cyrus met me on the street!"

Cyrus laughed but had the decency to apologise when Eve glanced furiously at him.

Ian hesitated. "Of course nothing is certain but..."

"But what? ..."

"I'm often right."

Eve almost laughed when she saw Cyrus and Zorfied vividly nodding.

Could be anyone with a badge. But she was not going to contradict him, after all, he was the one who was supposed to be a genius, and this could clearly help her find the killer.

Ian was looking at his notebook, hesitation showing on his face. "The last victim, I think I recognised her, I think she was working at the Gala ..."

Now that was something new, which indeed didn't bode well for the police.

"What do you mean?" Eve was bad with faces, especially women.

"I think she was one of the waitresses, but I still need confirmation." He nodded toward Zorf.

"I'm on it!"

Cyrus sighed. "What are the next steps?"

"We must prepare your statement on Monday. You too, Eve." Ian smiled. "Let's go home, you'll be safer."

Eve grimaced. She was tempted to say no and wait for the killer to come back. This time with knives tied to each of her limbs and traps set all around the flat. She wondered if he had followed her every move. If he had, it meant he had a little idea of her nocturnal expeditions, and that was of no help to Eve. So she was now officially competing with the police and Cyrus to find this killer.

Cyrus looked furious, and she was certain he would now put all his energy into finding him.

I've got to find him before my whole life goes to hell.

Chapter 19

Eve

The warm caress of the morning sun brought Eve out of her beauty slumber. She groaned, stretching her sore body, freezing when she realised she was not in her bed. Or in her bedroom. Memories of the previous night flooded back, and she sighed, accepting the potential trouble she was in. The police, her colleagues, were going to be on her back, certainly thinking they could protect her, but also probably categorising her in the "traitor" category. *Good times.*

Rising on her elbows, she took in the sight of Cyrus's spacious room, reflecting the man's larger-than-life persona. The bed, draped with Bordeaux curtains, resembled the dreamy princess beds she used to beg her parents for as a child. Two gigantic windows led to balconies, with what looked like a view of the manor's garden. The room contained cluttered bookshelves, teeming with dusty volumes, and an old couch facing a simple and tiny TV for the size of everything else in this room.

Though not extravagant, it was a perfect reflection of Cyrus, she sure was glad to know he could read.

Eve jumped in surprise as the bedroom door opened, , still groggy, but relaxed when she saw Cyrus in the door's frame, appearing to have come from the gym. Clad in a sweat-drenched grey t-shirt, his grey sweatpants NOT hiding much of his penis. Despite her sleepy head, and her thoughts of last night's events, Eve couldn't help but feel the familiar tingle in her body, and sent a thank you prayer to the Grey Sweatpants Gods.

She was enjoying the view when Cyrus silently crossed the room. Eve had to stop thanking whoever invented grey sweatpants to focus on his strange attitude.

Now that she was thinking about it, he hadn't spoken much the previous evening either. To be fair it was late, and they just came back here, changed, and went to bed. Her head still hurting like hell, she had appreciated that he didn't push for sex. But come on guy, she was wide awake now, and ready for some action!

"Are you grumpy?" she asked, straightforward. No time to lose beating around the bush.

Cyrus turned to her, scoffed, and removed his t-shirt, further fuelling her morning desire.

"What makes you think I am?"

"You literally didn't say a word after we left my flat, which is quite unusual seeing how you love hearing your own voice. And you were kind of acting like a dick."

Cyrus looked at her, surprised. Eve was pretty sure nobody had ever dared told him he acted like a dick. "Nah you know what? I don't care. Just stay in your grumpy mood. I just want sex, you don't need to talk, and we don't need to bond. And I certainly didn't sign up for a grumpy guy, before any sort of coffee."

Anger was making her French accent stronger than ever, which made her even more upset. The worst thing for him right now would be to ask her to repeat anything she said. She opened the covers and jumped out of the bed, trying to forget about the headache and the sore part of her head.

"Men!" she exclaimed, "And they say we are complicated!".

"Where do you think you're going?" Cyrus asked, walking toward her, still tranquil on the surface.

"I am going home." She took off her pyjama's and grabbed a clean silk maxi skirt and top. "Sun is shining, killer psycho is killing, and I am not gonna spend my weekend with your grumpy ass on my back."

Cyrus was standing to her side, arms crossed, looking at her while she was trying to brush her hair.

"No."

She stopped brushing, and turned to him, rage growing inside her. "No what??"

"You are not going home."

"Pleaaaase, stop me. Would love to see you try."

Cyrus scoffed and sported his sarcastic smile.

Eve finished packing the few things she had taken and walked to the door without looking at him. Before she could open the door, he pulled her away, pushing her towards it, her back hitting the door.

Cyrus blocked her with his body, kissing her with rage. Eve tried to get out of the kiss, still angry with him, but he swiftly moved her hands behind her back, pressing his body towards her. She could feel his erected penis, and was already wet for him, and would love to hate herself for it but she kissed him back.

His tongue forced passage into her mouth and Eve started moaning, she tried to take her arms back, but he was holding her firmly, devouring her mouth. Finally, he released her arms and grabbed her from under her butt, quickly throwing her on the bed after a few rapid steps.

Eve was breathless, laying on her back, watching the man push down his pants, freeing his dick, already hard and pulsing. His skin was shining from the light layer of sweat, and she felt the urge to take his perfect dick in her mouth again. Standing up, she was pushed without caution back to the bed again, the gesture was violent, he was, obviously, in some kind of grumpy state despite his negations.

He knelt above her tearing apart her top in a single move.

"What the fu-"

His mouth found her lips again, one hand catching her hands, positioning them together above her head, while his second hand went down, smoothly flying over her breast, before reaching the top of her skirt. Releasing Eve's hands for two seconds, he took away the soft piece of fabric and panties in a single movement, not hearing Eve's silent "thank you" for not tearing them apart. He took Eve's arms again and blocked them once more, this time using his t-shirt to tie her wrists together.

"Really?"

"Yep. You are not going anywhere before I make you scream my name."

Eve looked at him, standing over her, his dick pulsing and ready to take her. He could not stop gazing at her, full lust darkening his ocean eyes. She moved her hips forward, trying to make him understand it was time.

Cyrus shook his head and growled, finally penetrating her with a violent push, forcing his way into her tight pussy. Eve screamed, her head falling back, eyes closing, her pleasure mixed with pain under the forceful entry. He was not slow, and they started to let go of their accumulated tension.

His back and forth became more brutal, deeper, making Eve scream without restraint, her breath shattered by the violence of his thrusts. Cyrus's body crushed her, pounding her with all his strength, kissing her, varying the rhythm. Pulling out, pushing in, pinching her breast between his fingers or his teeth. He finally released Eve's arms from his bed and turned her over, pulling her back against his sweaty torso, wrists still tied. He caught her face between his hands and stole a kiss, thrusting back inside her, making her gasp in pleasure. He circled her throbbing clit with expert fingers.

The familiar wave reached her, stronger than ever, electrifying her entire body with desire, all while Cyrus took her mouth to its fullest, capturing her screams.

Eve crumbled on the bed when Cyrus finally let her go, trying to catch her breath when she felt his dick push against her ass. Eve groaned, trying to move her poor butt away from this giant stick but Cyrus grabbed her hips, pushing her body to the bed, keeping her flat.

He bent down, his lips on her ear. "Let me taste you. I want to taste every part of you. I can't wait to have a try at this perfect ass of yours."

Gosh he could almost make her blush. She turned her head as much as she could. "You are NOT going in with no preparation. Did you have a good look at your monster dick?"

Cyrus laughed. "Don't worry, Tiny Butt, I will be so gentle you will beg me to pay your ass a visit every single day."

"I'llbesogentleyouwillbegme" Eve grumbled, watching Cyrus heading for his bedside table, taking out what she guessed was lube.

"I sure hope this lubricants got some magical properties. Because I can tell you right now, THAT is not going to fit." She pointed as best as she could with her tied hands to his hardened penis. "I must have been crazy yesterday when I thought it could." Cyrus chuckled, and she bit her lips as he stroked himself, applying a generous amount of lube to his dick. *Man, he's hot. That's why I thought it would be fine yesterday.*

"Trust the process, Tiny Butt." He got on his knees, placing his mouth at her ass.

Moans quickly escaped Eve's mouth, his tongue playing her tight hole. She let out a scream when he spread her legs wider, giving him full access, she was feeling so exposed the simple idea of it was driving her wild. His tongue was insatiable, going in and out, sometimes getting lost on her clit, and was soon joined by a finger. Slowly at first, she contracted under the small intrusion, but mixed with Cyrus's other hand playing her like a guitar she quickly relaxed enough to enjoy the digit in her ass. Moans of pleasure escaped her, growing louder as the giant went faster, she gasped at the feeling of another finger joining the fun.

"For fuck's sake you are so tight I could come right now."

A depraved moan was the only answer. She felt his head coming back towards her ass, his hair tickling her hips and when his tongue joined his fingers Eve couldn't hold her pleasure, moving her body to get more of Cyrus's fingers and tongue, enjoying the feeling of him pulling her ass cheeks to clear a path for his incredible tongue.

"I'm curious to know if you are going to hump my dick the same way when I finally fuck you," he rasped, between tongues moves. "I can't wait anymore my Goddess, tell me you want me." He pulled Eve by her hair, eliciting a screaming of surprise, and without removing his fingers from her hole he kissed her, but stopped too fast for Eve's taste.

"Tell me, Eve, tell me where you want my dick right now," he whispered, nibbling her ear.

Eve's moans were getting out of control, she could feel her juice leaking all over her legs and she had only one wish. "Take me Cyrus, fuck my ass, make me yours again, as hard as you can."

"As you wish."

Cyrus

He pressed on her back pushing her down, adding a bit of the not-so-magical product on her entrance, and placed his dick against the most perfect ass he had ever seen. Despite Eve's request, he started slowly, more slowly than he ever would for another girl, he took his time, stretching her at first to be sure she would enjoy it. He was not stupid enough to be unaware of his size. But her body was welcoming him more than he thought, his lover perfectly relaxed, offering her tight hole for him to fuck.

A grunt emerged from Eve when he managed to get his entire tip inside her, she would need some time to get used to his presence. Eve's breath was heavy, he stroked her back, before playing a bit with her clit, instantly helping her relax more. Pushing further, Cyrus lost his mind, she was so tight the only thing he wanted to do was destroy her pretty ass; but as an anal lover, he knew that would sign the end of any ass-play later. And once again, he was too damn smart for that.

Finally they were able to find their rhythm, struggled growls replaced Eve's usual sounds of pleasure as Cyrus allowed himself to go deeper, faster, not giving her a second of rest. Moans became screams, thrusts got harder. Eve's face was ruined, tears pricking out of her eyes, grabbing the sheets as much as she could with her tied hands.

"Harder Cyrus, harder!" her raspy voice ordered, pushing her ass against him to take him as deep as possible.

"Jesus girl..." but he happily obliged, placing both hands on her hips, digging his fingers in the tender ass he loved, thrusting as hard as he could inside her, driving them to the edge.

Cyrus

A messy head full of curls was lying on him, right in the sweet angle at his shoulder, the one that makes every woman feel at home. Cyrus dropped his eyes on the woman sleeping against him, he was sure she was in Morpheus's world right now, not that he blamed her for it, he had never taken another woman as hard as he took Eve. *Genevieve.* What a funny name.

He raised his right hand to softly stroke her body and couldn't stop himself from grabbing a full fist of her ass, those peaches of hers were driving him crazy. Eve moaned, slapping his hand, chuckling.

Eve

"Don't you even think about it," she mumbled, without opening her eyes. A laugh answered her, and Eve felt movement from the heavy body of her lover, who swiftly positioned himself between her legs, his long hair falling above her, tickling her nose.

A kiss, soft and warm landed on her lips, and Eve took it all, Cyrus was for sure a great kisser, she may as well enjoy it while she was at it. The kiss stopped and Cyrus pulled back, mischievous light in his eyes.

"Did I finally manage to bring you to your knees, Tiny Butt? You sure know how to take a dick," his voice grew raspier on the last words and Eve could already feel his excitement growing close to her sex. Her fire was lit again, it was inhumane to get turned on with words.

"Sorry to disappoint, but you didn't," she teased, nibbling on his lower lips, then in a swift move she positioned herself on top of him, toppling the naked giant on his back. Damn he was heavy, but she didn't learn martial arts just to kill men. Well, she did, but she may as well use those skills for other stuff.

Surprised ocean eyes welcomed her, while she was laughing. "How in the living hell did you do that?" Cyrus laid still, taking in her naked body sitting on him right now. She moved her hips in a circle, her hands flat on his torso, keeping herself steady. Cyrus groaned when she moved her wet pussy above his dick, which was as usual ready for her. His eyes narrowed on her perky little pink nipples following the movement of her body, daring him to catch them between his teeth.

Eve leaned in, keeping the dance of her body, feeling the warmth of Cyrus against her clit. Without stopping she moved her mouth to his, biting his lips, inserting her tongue to play with his welcoming one, growls from the Neandertal answered her and she whined when she felt his hands grab at her ass.

"I'll never get enough of you," she whispered, her mouth moving close to his ear. "I'll never get enough of your dick ravaging me, of your tongue enslaving me. Of your fist destroying me." Without giving the man a second to answer, not that he could answer anything really, this was more of a statement, she impaled herself on his dick, hard as a rock and leaking so much cum already that she slid right onto it, barely feeling the pain, her pussy so drenched she was ready to take him all day.

Well, at least once, or maybe twice more.

A moan of pleasure was the only appropriate answer from Cyrus and while she was slowly sliding lower and lower, she could feel his eyes burning her, watching her sex spread over his gigantic dick. Cyrus closed his eyes when she reached the base, heavily breathing under the effort. She was so full now.

Cyrus

Their breathing accelerated as Eve reached a faster rhythm, whining and moaning under the pleasure and pain, the pain taking over for one tiny second when he grabbed her nipples between his index and thumb, twisting them as hard as he could, obtaining a raspy scream from Eve, and a drenched pussy getting even more hardcore on his dick.

The image of the brunette bouncing up and down on him, violently, deeply, all while having her tits tormented was driving him insane and Cyrus was trying his best to keep up, letting her have her orgasm before his.

"Come for me Goddess. Come so I can get you on your knees and fuck you as hard as I can again."

Only screams answered, Cyrus kept one hand on her breast, not stopping his torture, reaching the other to her throat, squeezing. Eve's face redden, her moans growing louder. She moved her hands onto his, squeezing.

"For fuck's sake girl..." he groaned, but obeyed, and was astonished by what he witnessed. A true Goddess, jumping and bouncing on his dick, not minding his size, not minding the pain, asking for more.

Eve's screams muffled by her throat squeezed, had Cyrus howling his pleasure, filling the room. Her juice ran all over him, and he wanted more, always more.

Chapter 20

Later that day that Eve and Cyrus got out of the comfortable bed, which definitely needed a change of sheets. Eve was starting to get "hangry," and she had to resort to threaten "no sex for the rest of the day" if he did not keep his promise of breakfast in bed.

She was glad she made a concession about the bed part though, now sitting in what Cyrus called pompously "the Breakfast Room." *Such a rich people thing to say.* But she sat quietly, blissful with admiration of the afternoon light hitting the oval-shaped room from every side possible. Windows covered maybe 90% of the walls, leaving few spaces for actual doors and walls, and whatever wall spaces left were skilfully carved with shapes of vines and flowers. The table in the middle was one of those old, fancy, stupidly long oak tables, but when she sat in one of the velvet-covered chairs, Eve felt like a princess.

She was busy testing the bounciness of the chair when a mocking laugh erupting behind her. Turning her head she spotted Cyrus, Ian, and Zorfied smiling at her.

"I would have thought you wouldn't be able to sit today..." Zorfied walked to Eve, daring to steal one of her croissants. With a scoff of outrage, she snatched back her piece of pastry.

"Why don't you worry about your ass instead, and DO NOT STEAL my croissant." Only laugher answered her remarks, food was sacred, and they were making fun of her??

"Excuse the lady, Zorf, she has a serious case of hanger apparently. Something about 'it's past 2pm and you still haven't fed me,'" Cyrus laughed, triggering expertly rolled eyes from his lover. He had placed his hand behind Eve's neck, leaning over her, discreetly controlling her head, forcing her to give him a croissant-kiss.

Eve sighed when the surprise kiss stopped and rolled her eyes one more time but didn't interrupt her consumption of the well-deserved breakfast. The man pulled a chair and sat beside her, leaving one of his hands hanging on her leg, softly stroking her.

A weird feeling invaded Eve, while she was busy devouring her butter croissant, something like weird tickles in her stomach was making her feel... uncomfortable? Were those butterflies? *Eeeeek!* Her sleepy-way-too-fucked mind was wrong, she didn't have butterflies in her belly.

Chewing slowly, she snuck a look towards Cyrus, who was laughing as usual with his gargantuan sound of a laugh to something stupid Zorfied said. He was indeed driving her a bit crazy, but once she saw past the typical Alpha male, she was finding it quite easy to let herself go with his flow, and his flow was an ocean during a storm. No wonder this man had broken hearts in the past, if even someone like her could start falling for him.

Eve couldn't stop a pout, letting her eyes enjoy the image in front of her, Cyrus was nonchalantly sitting, one hand on her leg, the other across the back of the chair, his legs spread, "manspreading," perfectly at ease here, in his house, surrounded by people he cared for. His black jeans hugged his legs, and with just a tiny bit of imagination Eve could guess the protuberance of her new favourite toy sitting under the fabric. The blue shirt opened slightly, let the top of his chest show, dark hair coming out. Forget about men and their smooth chest, all ridden of hair, as far as Eve was concerned there was nothing better than a hairy beast in her bed.

She had the decency to blush when Cyrus caught her looking at him, as a furrowed brow rose on his gorgeous face. She brought her little silver spoon to her mouth and gave it a lick, cleaning the delicious jam. Cyrus's eyes grew the dark shade that she had come to adore, the shade that screamed "you're gonna get fucked."

"Cyrus? Cyrus?"

Ian's voice was now just an echo and Eve from the corner of her eyes saw Cyrus's protuberance was now... well... protuberating. If that was a word. *Is it a word?* Cyrus's hand gripped her legs with a firm hold and with a smile he turned to his friends.

"Sorry Ian, I forgot Eve really wanted to see the hot pool."

Ian sighed, not duped for a second about any claimed visit to the hot pool. "We need to take the time to talk about your statement, this could get bad," he tried to argue, but it was a lost cause.

"Everything will be fine." Cyrus stood, and with no discretion at all readjusted himself. Eve threw him a warning look.

"I'm not done with my brekkie, sorry, the pool will have to wait." She gave Cyrus her naughtiest, dirtiest, sluttiest look, watching him from under her eyelashes.

She was picked up from her princess chair and thrown over a large shoulder under the laughs.

"Put me down" she screamed, holding back the laugh building inside her, but the only answer that came was a strong slap on her butt. She whined under the light strike of pain but didn't stop kicking, a bit of customary protest couldn't hurt, right?

A suite of white and black tiles soon gave way to an assemblage of mosaics, with no apparent structure or meaning but the random mix of colours. All shades of blue, it looked gorgeous, at least from where she was looking at it. She was abruptly dropped on the floor, thankfully feet first but she still thought it would be good measure to whine a bit stroking her stomach. She didn't have time to create a coherent sentence as Cyrus pushed on her shoulders. *Man he's strong.* Her legs ready to give up under the push.

"Yes Master?" She smiled. "How may I help you now?"

"Get on your knees." Cyrus's voice echoed in her ears, he was back to his raspy, insane sexy, "take me now" voice and it was driving her insane.

"Huuuum... I'm not sure, I just ate, I am feeling a bit full," Eve teased, waving her hand around his chest, opening his buttons one by one, languorously taking her time before reaching his leather belt. Cyrus chuckled, and after a fast intake of breath when Eve's hand brushed his boner, he pushed harder on her shoulders.

"I said, get. on. your. knees."

Eve gave him a naughty look, busy opening his pants to free him, while he took off his belt. She stopped, giving him a curious look, a smirky smile on her face.

"You are SO NOT whipping me with that." *I mean, maybe you could?*

"Who said anything about whipping?" He enclosed the leather around his hands and in a fast move placed the luxury leather against Eve's neck, encircling her fragile skin with his belt. Her breath became wheezy and to her shame the fire in her loins intensified under the pressure.

"Trust me." Cyrus gave her a final push to her knees, keeping a strong hold on the belt. Eve finally broke and felt the coldness of the mosaics touch her knees. Her hands encircled his large dick, playing with it, extracting pre-cum and a groan. Cyrus held his head a bit back, eyes closed, savouring the so needed touch.

"Uh uh Mr Get On Your Knees, if I am gonna suck your dick while you strangle me you are going to watch me."

Cyrus

Cyrus's laugh erupted in the room, but he brought his eyes to his lover, appreciating the view from above, her slutty hazel eyes looking at him from under her long eyelashes, her mermaid hair still damp from the shower spread around her shoulders. Her tits hanging out of her camisole were just waiting to be pulled and pinched, all pink and hard already.

"Open this sweet mouth of yours then," he murmured, placing his thumb in Eve's mouth, pulling on her bottom lip and teeth. Her tongue reached out when he brought his dick closer, before sliding inside her warmth, growling like a bear, his tip was in, but he wanted more.

Suction noise and excited whines from Eve mixed with the bubbly sound coming from the water beside them disturbing the peace of the pool room. Cyrus placed a hand behind her head pulling on the belt a bit stronger with the other.

"Take all of me Genevieve, or this will get tighter." He pulled on the leather, Eve's face reddening, her eyes full of tears, shadowed with desire. If he were to inspect her pussy, he would find a pool of cum down there. But it was not time yet, so he pushed himself harder inside her tight mouth, holding her head with such a grip Eve had no choice but to take him all. His groans grew louder as she struggled under the push, tears running freely on her cheeks, but she was happily accommodating his dick, moving her mouth along the full-length, all while caressing his balls.

"My God you're such a good girl, do you know that?" Cyrus whispered, giving her some air, releasing the tight belt just a bit. She gave him a naughty look and without stopping moved a hand to the belt, tightening the leather around her neck.

This simple action was too much for Cyrus to handle, and with some wild animal growls he accelerated his movement, forcing her head along his dick, listening to her gurglings and whines until he finally came, howling his pleasure inside her. The ejaculation must have taken her by surprise, Eve had a funny look, and unlike usual she was letting some of the cum escape her mouth.

Cyrus chuckled. "Sorry my Goddess, you kind of drove me surprisingly crazy there." He took a step back, fully enjoying the view in front of him, Eve was looking at him, mouth slightly open, cum dribbling along her chin, dropping on her tits, hands on her knees trying to get her breathing back to normal.

Laughing, she stood struggling to be caught by strong arms, stopping her ankylosed legs fully giving up under her. Picking her up, he stabilised her in his arms, placing his right hand under her knees and the other under her arms, then without a word he took her towards the well-deserved hot pool, all bubbly and warm.

Swiftly he took off her camisole and her skirt, noticing the missing underwear with a chuckle, wondering if she just forgot to wear it today, before he softly dropped her in the water, enjoying the view of her relaxed body covered in his various light bruises.

Eve

Eve always loved hot pools, and spas, and saunas, she was a fucking lizard. And feeling the warmth of the water against her hurt body was the best feeling ever. Well not quite. She closed her eyes, listening to clothes being dropped on the floor. Then opened her eyes just enough to see Cyrus getting in the pool, enjoying the full front naked Cyrus, rolling her eyes when she saw his elephant dick back to pointing up.

"Don't worry love." Cyrus sat beside her, lifting her to place her on his body, allowing her head to lay back on the strong chest. "I think someone deserves the best orgasm of her life right now." Eve moaned loudly as his hands followed the contour of her breast heading south. A sweet little finger session was all she needed right now.

"You bet I do." She whined when she felt a slow pinch on her clitoris. Rotating her head slightly she caught Cyrus's heavy look and whispered. "But as soon as I am back on my feet, per se, I want you to fuck my ass while holding this damn belt of yours around my neck."

152

Chapter 21

Eve

A bad case of the Mondays, added to the question of whether Eve still had a job, even if as far as she was concerned she was the victim. She wasn't sure if she should be concerned or not about the lack of news from Erik or Andy. If you forgot about the long text message requesting her presence for her statement. To be fair she had been quite busy getting her brain fucked out by Cyrus. Brain, pussy, ass, mouth, who cares about the details.

Meanwhile, her giant had been formally summoned, an official convocation arriving for him by special courier pretty please. Ian temporarily diverted his attention from the psychopath case to prepare their arguments, ready to confront the detectives head-on. As he said so well, "We can't afford to waste time on their stupid inquiries." Not to mention that not long-ago Erik and many policemen were all agreeing about Cyrus's innocence. This looked like they needed a guilty man to satisfy everyone in Ireland, and Cyrus was the perfect choice.

Eve, Cyrus, Ian, and Zorfield rode in Cyrus's car, Eve not sure why Zorfied felt he had to come. Probably just in it for the fun, though she had thought he could be here as some kind of bodyguard. But the thought of Cyrus having a bodyguard was ridiculous.

Zorfield drove, not as smoothly as Cyrus, while Ian sat to his side rereading his notes, a hand on his partner's thigh. He had once again put on his serious attire, hair tidy, gorgeous costume.

Eve and Cyrus were in the back, Cyrus right by her side, his hands gently tracing her leg. Eve looked at the landscapes passing before her eyes but not really seeing them, so lost in her thoughts. She had tried to think all night about what she could say to Erik, how to explain the "itsy bitsy mini" presence of Cyrus in her life.

Erik was not only her boss, but she also truly considered him a rare friend and she couldn't help but feel a bit guilty about hiding her kind-of-relationship with Cyrus. It wasn't like she hadn't been warned not to get too close to McRory. No, oh no, she had plenty of warnings and an entire set of bells begging her to stop.

Her new goal in life was to stop attracting unwanted attention, especially from her colleagues. She had been quick thinking enough to copy all information regarding the murders before the events of the past weekend, those coupled with Ian's guesses in the investigation certainly gave her the means to get to the killer before the police. And hopefully before Cyrus. Even if the perspective of Cyrus kicking the psycho's ass was getting her more turned on then it should. She was glad the weekend went without anymore of grumpy Cyrus, but brave as she was she didn't ask him what the hell was wrong with him, after all who doesn't like a bit of make-up sex?

Her primary concern was shutting off the other psycho before he could reveal any of her nocturnal activities. Her plan was to play bait, and test Ian's theory about her being the target. She would be a prepared, ready to kick ass bait, and this freaking psycho would never see her coming.

Mwaahmwaaahmwaaaah.

Cyrus's hand tightened on her thigh, and she sighed. *This is not going to be easy.* She turned her head to look at him, already showing his naughty smile, looking at her with fire in his eyes. She instantly regretted her outfit, her favourite green ribbed long dress, a dress which was now being lifted with curiosity by Cyrus's sneaky hand. Thankfully, they arrived at the station before the man could do anything stupid, like getting a bit too close to her burning core. The team parked in the underground garage and got out of the car, walking towards the lift entrance.

Ian stopped everyone. "Cyrus let Eve go inside without you holding her."

Cyrus scoffed and grabbed Eve's hips in a possessive manner, his arm almost encircling her.

"Seriously Cyrus, don't make it harder. We are going to be under fire. Especially Eve." Eve couldn't see Ian's face, but she guessed he was most likely using his world-famous disapproving look. She started twisting her head to check if she was right, but Cyrus's mouth hit hers, stealing a deep, warm kiss, letting his hand venture south, brushing her ass.

Eve's heart raced and she sighed squirming around to get rid of Cyrus's arm. "You guys are going to do just fine; I am the one getting fired."

Without listening to his complaints, she hurried and pushed the heavy window door. Entering the reception area, she spotted the two policemen behind the desk looking at her before exchanging a knowing look, eyebrows raised. But she ignored them, rumours and gossip were the least of her worries right now.

They entered onto the ground floor, and Eve saw Erik and the dick Cragnum upstairs, acting as if they were waiting for her at the door to her office, both their arms crossed over their chest. She breathed deciding to stop by Andy and Bonnie to check how bad the situation was.

"You are in deep shit girl." Andy almost sounded like he thought the situation was funny.

"This is not funny Andy, we really didn't need that." Bonnie looked at Eve and whispered, "Erik is in trouble, you are in trouble. All of this because you could not resist Cyrus."

"That's unfair Bonnie," Eve whispered back. "And you said it yourself, he is not as bad as people say." Her argument was bad, but she was desperate.

"Yes, and what did I add after that??" the brunette retorted, storm in her eyes.

That I should stay away. Pouting, Eve turned her head to have a look at her boss, trying to judge how angry exactly he was with her.

Cyrus and his friends walked around the place as if nothing bad happened, acting as if they possessed the station. Which from what Eve heard, was almost the case. Every single policeman and woman were looking at the group now, voices murmuring. Eve was pretty sure they weren't talking about her assault, but more about why in the hell she would be stupid enough to get with Cyrus. To be fair, she asked herself the same question every day. But it was usually followed by images of Cyrus's dick thrusting into her.

She moved as Andy and Bonnie started getting up. "We are doing Cyrus's deposition." Bonnie shrugged. "And Cragnum is going to watch."

Eve scoffed. "This guy was not that interested in the killing until Cyrus eventually got involved."

Bonnie exchanged a look with her partner, they both knew. Everyone knew actually, but if there was a tiny reason to give trouble to Cyrus, any Commander should be onto it, it was only fair after all.

They reached the bottom of the stairs leading to Eve's office, poor Eve trying to hide as much as possible behind the Dynamic Duo, but it was harder than it looked. Andy grabbed her wrist, pulling her close, his lips barely moving to her ear. "They really think your boyfriend attacked you."

Eve stood back, surprised. "Really?" she whispered back. The Detective nodded, and then with a head sign to Cyrus, he advised him to follow.

The giant's jaw was tight, his eyes dark with fervour, looking at Eve's wrist where Andy held her. Eve rolled her eyes at him, mouthing "behave" before turning back and spotting Erik at the top of the stairs.

He looked down on his assistant gesturing her to come with his finger. Eve sighed, and put her foot on the first step but Cyrus's large hand held her back, she turned away, ready to give him the big eyes, again, but was immediately trapped by the giant's mouth on hers, AGAIN.

Eve pushed Cyrus away. "You are NOT helping, Cyrus."

"You don't need help." He caught her hand and gave her a chaste kiss while smiling sarcastically.

Eve let out a loud sigh, but felt those awful butterflies in her stomach again, and finally managed to reach Erik. Her friend was looking more tense than ever, his eyes shining behind his glasses, jaw clenched, not a hint of a smile on his lips. Cragnum was, for himself, smiling, more of a smirk, but still, it was quite disturbing, and Eve wished she never saw it.

She tilted her head. "Let's finish this quickly, after all you have a killer to catch, seeing that you let him go Saturday." Her last comment was unfair, but she knew they were going to blame her one way or another anyway.

"Well, the killer is right where he is supposed to be." Cragnum pointed toward Cyrus with his bobbly chin. "And Erik and I are both going to enjoy taking your deposition as well, so many unknowns in this story."

Eve couldn't help but let a crystalline laugh out. *So, Andy was right.* Cragnum truly thought Cyrus attacked her despite her initial statement.

"Yeah sure, whatever. Don't you want to hear what Cyrus has to say? Or do you prefer annoying me with your stupid theories?" She was feeling fully uninhibited now and didn't really care anymore. She technically could not be more in trouble besides losing a friend. They had nothing on her — *I sure hope so* — nothing on Cyrus.

Cragnum frowned his fluffy eyebrows, upset. "I will listen to him, he is just gonna need to wait till I am done with you first."

"I am sure that's gonna make him happy," Eve asserted. After all, Cyrus was not known for being the most patient guy in the room.

Walking at fast speed out of what used to be her office, Eve's heart raced as she finally left the witch hunt she just went through. Erik and Cragnum's accusatory words echoed in her mind as she quickly walked down the stairs, her thoughts swirling with frustration and determination.

As expected, they had tried to pin the blame squarely on Cyrus, who was such a convenient suspect. But Eve wasn't about to back down, and she spent the last hour trying to put some sense into Cragnum's little head, and to her dismay into Erik's as well. She had thought Erik would believe her, after all he said it himself, Cyrus was not a psychopathic killer-rapist; but he seemed to have lost all kind of say in the police now and had stayed silent the whole time. And she knew she was responsible for it. Leaning against the cold corridor wall once out of view from those damn gossip boys at the front desk, she gathered her thoughts, remembering how hard she fought for Cyrus in there. *Damn those butterflies.*

She and the boys knew it was going to be a long shot, but she needed the police to understand there was more to the story, but at least she said what she had to say, her only hope was for the actual detectives to keep going on the true killer, she knew Andy and Bonnie would not give up until they had the actual killer behind bars.

She had recounted the details of Ian's theory to her superiors, and the more she talked the more she could see they were both quite adamant the killer could not be part of their perfect little world. She wondered why she was even surprised about that, even she at first had entirely refuted Ian's theory. Nobody likes to think their colleagues, their friends could be responsible for such horrendous crimes. Her judges had exchanged sceptical glances, and tension had escalated quickly. And now she was out of a job. Cragnum even dared mentioning she was not that interesting to get a stalker after her.

Eve scoffed, she was hot, wasn't she? Of course men would go around and slaughter women who looked like her, it was not THAT weird. Her breath now normal, she dried her tears of rage and frustration and stormed out the door, Zorfield, rushing to her side. Eve then understood why he was there. Of course, Cyrus must have thought she needed a bodyguard after her misadventure. She turned to him, her eyes blazing with defiance.

"I need some time alone, Zorfield," she asserted, her voice resolute. "I can't think straight."

Zorfield's brow furrowed, a slight concern on his face.

"Hum, nah." He took out a cigarette from his pocket, ready to light it. "Cyrus would get my fucking balls if I let you go, and I love my balls."

Eve sighed. "I'll be careful. I just need some air."

"Ok, how about I drive you home, but I stay at the door... eh? Cy is a bit scared you're gonna go all bait and stuff with the killer."

Eve scoffed. *How the hell did he guess that?*

"Fine but you stay outside ok? I'll deal with Cyrus."

"Sure he would love that," Zorfield laughed.

They quickened their pace to reach the dim lit carpark, Zorfield reaching for his keys in his back pocket.

Something feels off...

She turned around just in time to see Zorfield stumbling backward, his eyes wide with shock. Before she could react, a sharp blow struck the back of her head, and darkness closed in around her. This was becoming a habit she would happily do without. Before her consciousness fully went out, blurrying vision at its best, she spotted not one, but two pair of shoes standing in front of her.

Fear clutched at Eve's chest, heart poundin in her ears. *We were fucking wrong.* Not one, but two.

I hate team games...

Chapter 22

Cyrus

Cyrus was done with the interrogation already. He had heard Eve's heels click on the stairs a few minutes ago and knew she was out of her, probably storming outside, Zorf after her as he instructed him to do. The giant sighed, rolled his eyes while looking at an invisible point on the ceiling. He was used to being called by the police, and he knew what to answer and how to behave; leaving the biggest part of the job to Ian.

Andy and Bonnie were done with the situation too, he could see it on their faces. Bonnie was now throwing dark looks towards Cragnum, who had joined them as soon as Cyrus had heard Eve leaving. Erik was nowhere to be seen. Even Andy, who was glooming earlier, threatening Cyrus with random accusations, was now sitting on his chair, grumpy that Cragnum took charge.

"Your girlfriend told us many things, Cyrus," Cragnum started, a light in his eyes.

That made Cyrus laugh, to Cragnum's anger. This kind of pseudo intimidation would never work on him, especially when, for once, he had nothing to do with the murders.

Ian jumped in. "I'm guessing you're talking about my discoveries? I prepared a beautiful profile for your team this weekend." Ian may be shy most of the time, but when it came to his job, he was in his elements, able to destroy anyone with any words.

Cragnum's big brows formed a V, but Andy interrupted him, now at the edge of his chair. "Which profile?"

Ian smiled. "The one which tells you where to look for the killer. In here."

Andy muttered a "What", but Cragnum interrupted him.

"This is bullshit. This is you trying to get your friend out of this shit! No police officer under MY orders would be so low as to slaughter people."

"You think it's one of us?" Bonnie asked, her eyes bright, gripping her pen.

"Probably. And the last victim? I just had confirmation this morning. She was a waitress at your gala."

Cragnum sighed, opening his mouth to speak.

"We had cameras at the manor!" Andy spoke, excitation showing in his voice, and he was already getting up. "The owner was grumpy at the party from two years ago, someone had taken a shit in the library."

Cyrus raised an eyebrow. Eve would not be happy about the camera thing, but the owner of the Manor was for sure going to enjoy his time watching the recordings.

"You did?" asked Ian, now getting up as well. "Andy, we need to check those NOW."

Cragnum was trying to speak above all the overly excited chatter in the room, his bushy eyebrows moving up and down in rhythm with his fury, when Detective Mark rushed into the room without knocking, to everyone's stupefaction. His face was red, and he was sweating as if he had run.

Mark threw a look at Cyrus, then at Ian, swallowing. "He took her. He took Eve. And we had to call an ambulance to take Zorfied to the hospital,"

Cyrus instantly stood, his body trembling as he threw the chair around, furry running through his veins.

"WHO??

"You're not gonna believe it—"

"Mark! out!" Cragnum stormed between them. "Everyone that is not part of this interrogation just needs to…"

But Cyrus was already moving, Ian following, and without more thought he pushed Cragnum aside.

"WHO??"

"Johnny, one of our cops," Mark sighed. "I was heading out for a smoke when I saw Zorf on the floor and Johnny loading Eve into a car. He took off before I could get to them" Mark barely had time to finish his sentence, Cyrus and Ian already through the door, followed closely by Andy and Bonnie, all ignoring Cragnum raging behind them.

They ran to the garage, where cops were on the site, grouping around an immobile mass being moved to an ambulance. Cyrus caught Ian's hand and with determination they advanced towards it, his platinum spiky hair covered with blood, paramedics hovering over him.

"You go with him." Cyrus nodded, and before Ian could protest he pushed him in the ambulance.

"You go with him, I'll get Andy to check the manor's cameras to confirm this is the guy. I need to stay here with Bonnie to make sure they make a proper search."

He turned towards both Detectives and saw Andy ready to protest against being ordered around.

"I need you Andy," Cyrus said, a slight beg in his voice.

The two men exchanged a look.

"Fine, but you aren't the boss of me!" Andy took a break. "I'll go check the cameras and Bonnie can help you here." Before Cyrus could even laugh at him, the detective turned on his heels, his phone already out in his hand.

164

Chapter 23

Eve

The unmistakable smell woke up Eve, a mouldy, fishy odour she was all too familiar with. The realisation hit her like a jolt: she was aboard a boat, but the quiet sound of the boat surfing the waves made her guess she was not en route to the open sea, yet.

Just great. Her head was throbbing stronger than the last attack, the dry blood stuck to her scalp, pulling on her hair. This dick didn't miss. Despite the nagging ache in her head, she tried to assess her situation.

She was naked and really not happy about it. She turned her head to the side, pulling a face when the sore on her head disagreed with the movement.

Her tender wrists were secured to a wooden cross in the shape of an 'X.' On the plus side, her feet remained free — a small comfort in her current circumstances but she would take anything positive she could.

Glancing around the unpleasant cabin, she deduced it seemed to belong to some sort of small fishing vessel, maybe even a personal boat. Hence the disgusting odour. Except sushi, Eve didn't like to eat fish, and she hated this smell.

She tried to move her hands, but her efforts were met with a numbness indicating she had likely been in this position for some time. Her upper body screamed its discomfort, but despite her lousy situation she came to hope Zorfield was still alive and that the boys were looking for her. She would never forgive herself if Zorfield died because of her, not that she would survive much longer in the company of the killer. Killers.

Riiiight. Two pairs of shoes. She let out a frustrated growl. They caught her before she could be a prepared bait, not fair. Which kind of serial killer does that?

The only door in the room creaked open, the rusted metal opening with difficulty, revealing a tall, fat, well known grouper-face. Eve couldn't hold back a disdainful snort. *Johnny.* He appeared even worse than in her memory, his outfit made of a have-know-better-days tank top and grey sweatpants covered in various stains, showing his boner underneath.

The Gods of Grey Sweatpants should have put some rules about who is allowed to wear those.

"Fantastic," she muttered, the fear growing inside her turning to shame. Shame that this grouper guy swam right under her nose all this time and she didn't spot him for what he was.

Before she could say a word, gathering all her collection of best insults, a second figure joined their little party. Standing in the shadows of the door, his voice resonated in the room, chillingly familiar.

"Hello, Eve," he purred.

It felt as though her heart was being ripped out of her chest, leaving a hole in what used to be her body.

"Erik?" Eve asked, barely recognising her own voice "What the fucking hell??"

She tried to move pulling on her ropes, furious at him, but more important-ly, furious at herself for failing to detect his psychopathic side during all their years of friendship. *Does Mira know? Is he hurting her as well and I didn't see it?*

Erik advanced towards Eve, while Johnny placed a leather case on the table, meticulously revealing its contents one by one, giggling at every new tool. Eve pouted, being the torturer was way more fun than being the torturee.

Ok quick quick, make them talk, classic but efficient. Her thoughts rushed through her mind, hoping Cyrus and especially Ian would be smart enough to pinpoint who the fuck the killer was. *Killers.* Damn, she would never get used to that.

"Erik, I need to know why, what happened?" she begged, watching him move closer to her, examining her naked offered body.

The man scoffed. "Trying to win some time, Eve? Really?"

Yes you idiot, I read many thrillers.

"You know how curious I am, I think I'm owed a fucking explanation," she whined unable to hold back her repulsion when Erik positioned his hands over hers, slowly moving them over her body, squeezing any bit of flesh he could.

"More," he whispered.

"...More ... what?" she whimpered when he painfully squeezed her nipples, rotating them in such an unnatural way she thought he would rip them off. A shiver raced through her, a surge of fear rushing through her body. Images of previous victims crashed into her mind, she knew what these two men were capable of, and she was not going to have any kind of fun right now.

He finally released her breast, standing there looking at her in disgust.

"More of everything darling." He glanced at Johnny and nodded in confirmation when Johhny showed him something in his hand. "I hadn't done anything before I met you, was just living my life, with my boring wife, my boring job. The only highlight was when some fascinating killers were active, I wanted to catch them, not to punish them, but to UNDERSTAND them. To know how it felt to be rid of all judgement, to just do whatever you wanted, without hearing whiny protests from my wife or some random whore. When I met you, I wanted to fuck you. Obviously."

"Obviously," Eve mumbled.

"But you didn't show any kind of interest for me, and well, Mira was there anyway."

Eve's heart quickened as Johnny approached her with a shiny scalpel. She tried to not look at their erections as a retching took her by surprise, she, who was usually more than resistant.

"Then, war happens." Erik smiled. "Ah the war, Eve, it was marvellous."

"Marvellous is not the term I would have chosen."

"Come on, I know you had your fun too, we all did, even Cyrus you know. He always liked the blood." Erik stopped, his eyes seeming to look at an ancient memory. "It changed us, all of us, more or less. And some of us, like you and I, we took such a liking to killing. We never truly stopped. Right?"

So he knew about her extra-curriculum activities. Nothing surprising in that, but still, this was upsetting. *Sure hope the Guild never learn this.*

"We.Are.Not.The.Same."

"Well, you kill men, I kill women. You aren't the tenderest murderer you know. Slashed penis? Really?"

"I am PUNISHING men, assholes really, I am not raping them and torturing them for no reason."

"Does that make you sleep better at night to think that?" Erik mocked.

"Actually yes it does, thanks for asking." She was not a psychopath, he was!

Fury boiled inside her when both men heartfully laughed. That's why she was killing men, because they were all fucking annoying. *Except maybe three.*

Erik stopped laughing. "Anyway, you know what we do to our little friends, we may cut you a bit, but we are gonna fuck you so much, and so hard, you will wish we just killed you." He leaned in close, smirking. "Do you want to know what our favourite part is? I was not a big fan at first, but the feeling of it, God, that's the best. I let Johnny fuck your pussy while I take your ass, and seeing how you seem to handle Cyrus, I am sure you will enjoy yourself. Slut one day, slut every day." Erik smirked. "I am so glad I placed cameras in your flat before I rented it to you."

That explains a lot.

She didn't take her gaze off his for a second as Johnny brought the blade to her cheek nor did she make a sound as the bladed slash her skin, running down the length of her cheek, hot blood rushing, flowing from the raw wound.

"Not the face you fucking idiot," Erik growled. "You know I don't like uglies."

"Sorry boss," Johnny chuckled, his laugh causing Eve another retch. She quickly forgot about it when the scalpel went down, following the shape of her chin, her neck, her clavicle, cold metal against her frozen skin.

"Thanks to me at least Johnny here is ameliorating his taste. He killed the prostitute first you know, I was not there. She was not that pretty. And she was fat, I don't like fatties either, I got one at home already."

Johnny mumbled something, still playing with his scalpel.

"He made a mistake that day, didn't you Johnny?" Erik asked, watching Johnny from above his glasses.

"Yeah boss."

"That's how I found him. Here he was, like me, easy to convince to get better. So when you accepted my offer, oh Eve, how glad we were. Johnny here even brought your picture home. Of course I was a bit surprised when I learned you were going around killing some randoms... that changed our plans a bit."

"Fucking psychopaths." Eve rolled her eyes.

She took a deep breath, ready for the pain when Johnny moved the scalpel to her right breast. Her lips pinched when he started cutting, deepening the blade in her soft curve, going down further, almost to her nipple. The pain was so strong tears welled in her eyes, she didn't want to give them the satisfaction of begging, but this was the worst pain she had ever been through, and it was just starting.

Erik continued, though, she would have rather have him without her being sliced open, this was not how winning time was supposed to work.

"Then both together, it was easy, so easy. Johnny would use his uniform to get the girls to open their door, they never saw us coming. When we learned Roisin was one of Cyrus's conquests, we thought we may as well try to pin it on him, Cragnum was so gullible he went with it. We didn't even plan it, but Cyrus is such a fuckboy it was easy to find previous partners."

"Ok stop talking now." Eve breathed, watching the scalpel destroy her. Tears running down her cheeks, she moved her head aside, not ready to watch her breast being cut in half, then she saw him. A shadow jumped into the room, pushing Erik out of the way, throwing him against the mouldy wall with a bang, knocking him out. Johnny still under the shock of Cyrus's arrival, gave Eve the chance to put her last strength together and raise her legs, catching him in a choke between her tights, squeezing, focused on annihilating him. It took longer than necessary, her strength not at her best right now, and she didn't stop when Cyrus came to her after checking on Erik, watching her. Murdering. That's what she was best at. But she didn't care.

Exhausted she finally released Johnny's body, and it fell on the floor like the slug he was. Her legs shook, her entire body so weakened by the cold that she didn't protest when Cyrus tenderly cut her ties, and she collapsed onto him, her face drenched by what she thought was sweat, was actually tears. Eve sniffled, grasping her lover's neck with her weakened arms, letting him take her away from the nightmare. He gently placed his leather coat on her naked body, but it didn't stop the shivering.

They walked past an unconscious Erik but ignored him.

"The Duo is on their way." Cyruswent first through the narrow door and helped Eve climb the two steps. He reached the side of the boat, pulling back the gangway to allow them to walk out when Eve felt a sharp pain in her back, she tried to turn, wincing under the cold metal.

"Cyrus!" she called, now perfectly awake. Erik held her, his ragged breath in her ear, his arm surrounding her throat, a knife now pointing straight at her eye, threatening Cyrus to make a move.

Cyrus turned on his heels, his eyes blazing with fury, his fist clenched by his side.

"Not a move Cyrus, or she loses her pretty eye." Erik walked them backward towards the guardrail, instinctively trying to put some distance between the giant and himself, too bad he didn't consider who the biggest threat on this boat was.

Eve clenched her body.

"It's not him you should be afraid of, Erik."

In a swift movement she had blocked his hand holding the scalpel and gave him a hard, nose-breaking headbutt. Feeling his imbalance she pushed on her legs, knocking them into the water, listening to Cyrus's furious calls.

She knew her body was weak, but she also knew in water, there was no man who could stand a chance against her. She used to freedive with sharks for fuck's sake, Erik forgot that. As soon as their bodies entered the frozen water, she felt him panicking behind her. She rotated in the water like a mermaid, her limbs floating naturally in the dark water and saw the shadow in front of her already struggling to reach back to the surface, his coat and shoes slowing him down, his nose bleeding all around him. Eve propelled herself towards him, he had lost his knife in the process and had no way to protect himself. She caught him between her legs, surroundings his thick waist, holding him and reached for his face, placing her thumbs on his eyes, pushing, squeezing, listening to the beautiful gargling sounds coming out of his mouth. Maybe he would even drown before his eyeballs exploded. Who knows.

With satisfaction she felt the budge of his eyes receding under her push, his hands tentatively trying to push her, but it was too late. A few more seconds and she knew he was gone, two bleeding orbits in place of his eyes.

Eve let his body float away, bringing herself back to the surface, surprised Cyrus didn't jump in to rescue her. She let out a long breath when she was finally out of the water, and she saw Cyrus.

"You jerk!" The man was peacefully observing her, his elbows on the guardrail, a smirk on his mouth.

"You seemed to have this specific situation under control," he retorted, and for good measure he threw her one of the rescue buoys.

Chapter 24

Eve

Two days later, and after an intense interrogation Eve and Cyrus emerged from the police station, tired and groggy, flanked by the ever-loyal Ian, who had still maintained his facade as their lawyer just in case. The weight of the recent events hung in the air, palpable and unspoken.

Andy and Bonnie had endured the gruelling process of taking their depositions, their expressions revealing the shock still gripping them. *Didn't see that one coming.* It was more than just solving a case, it was finding out that one of the people you trusted the most in this world was a monster.

Outside the station, journalists were already buzzing around. An "anonymous" tip had been received, implicating the Commander and an unfamiliar officer as the two psychopaths behind the murders. Zorfield was quite bored at the hospital and thought it would be funny to throw some gas on the never-ending fire.

Hopefully this will keep them busy a while, Eve thought, not forgetting her own troubles that came with her particular hobby.

Zorfield was waiting at the car, a proud smirk directed at the hive of reporters. Eve was so glad he had been found alive and well.

Eve would have much rather kept everything silent and just burned the damn boat and body, "no body, no crime," but her and Cyrus didn't have time to think about it with the Dynamic Duo already on site. Eve wasn't the kind to cry a lot, but when Bonnie rushed to her, hugging her tightly in her mist of orange and cinnamon smell, she felt the tears flow freely unable to fight them.

Too bad her misadventure didn't help the whole "you're fired" situation. According to Cragnum the fact that her boss was a psychopath apparently didn't compensate her lack of duty and the shame of her relationship with Cyrus. The same Cragnum who had been glowing with joy when he saw her leaving the station with a box of her stuff. He didn't seem to care much for her various bruises, and at her surprise, didn't care much about the two bodies left behind. Eve's guts were screaming that Cyrus had something to do with that.

But it was still satisfying to see Cragnum step out of the station, his eyes scanning the crowd of journalists, to then yell at the poor policeman on duty. "Who the hell tipped off those fuckers??" Cragnum's gaze shifted towards Cyrus and his friends, who stood a short distance away, and Eve could see his furrowed brows raise in anger as he watched Zorfield playfully showing him his phone.

Eve's lips curled into a wry smile as she observed the hordes of eager journalists swarming. She spotted Andy and Bonnie peaking their head out the front door before heading back inside, neither were big fans of journalists. She joined them in a few steps, Andy was grumpy as usual, but Bonnie had tears in her eyes. She caught Eve's hand, holding it for a few seconds.

"You take care of yourself chica, and if this big boy is annoying you—" she moved her chin towards Cyrus "—you come and talk to me."

That made Eve laugh, that was a fight she would love to watch, she threw herself at the Detective and hugged her. "Bye guys, sorry for the trouble".

Andy groaned. "You're lucky you almost fucking died or else I would kick your ass."

Eve chuckled, and without further ado she went to her boys, waiting to escort her home. She wanted to stop first by her flat, mostly to pick up some clean clothes, but also her weapons. Some deep instinct was screaming to her she was going to need them.

Head laying on the top of her seat, watching landscapes transforming from buildings to grass and rivers, Eve was finally resting, she had been given an insane amount of pain pills for her cut and was feeling high. Ian was behind the wheel, while Zorfield's bandaged head rested on his seat. Poor Zorfield attempted a conversation as the car started moving forward but he gave up quickly at the heavy ambiance in the small space. Turned out even he knew when to stop.

Back at the mansion, Cyrus wasted no time marching straight in, leaving Eve and the others behind. During the half-hour drive, he hadn't uttered a word, leaving an uneasy feeling in Eve's stomach. He had spent some time at the hospital with her but not as much as she would have liked, and she hated herself for it. She would have appreciated a bit more care following the tough days she had, and Cyrus's coldness was flipping her stomach, agitating the butterflies inside. She knew he was busy with covering Erik and Johnny murders and stuff, but still.

Eve sighed, turning to Ian for answers. "What in the hell is he in a bad mood for? We're alive!" Which as far as she was concerned, was the best news of the day.

"Maybe it's best you ask him directly. He'll be in the gym, venting on a poor sandbag." Ian's emerald eyes shone in the late afternoon sun, a knowing light in them.

Before heading to the gym, Eve felt she needed something as a safety measure prior to facing him, and started climbing the stairs leading to Cyrus's room with determination. Something was up and her instincts had rarely steered her wrong.

Let's not mention the whole Erik and Johnny situation thing, thank you very much.

She was now scared Cyrus knew about her whereabouts and hobby, she was rewinding the movie of the last 48hours in her head and the possibility that Cyrus heard her spilling the beans about her passion for murder. At the hospital he spoke quickly about how they found her, and once they could spot Johnny on the videos from the gala it was quite easy to put one and one together. It was his boat. Cyrus asked Ian to distract the Duo long enough to give him an advance and he had hurried to rescue her. Cyrus was not exactly an angel either, but he was not like her, going around and slashing dicks because he enjoyed it.

A smart serial killer now would just run away, take a plane, and hide. Hide very well. But the idea of having someone like Cyrus, with his means and his damn stubbornness, chasing her for the next few months or years was not as enticing as it sounded. Besides, she was not that smart.

She swiftly changed into a more suitable attire, slipping into a pair of yoga pants and her favourite wrists weapons. Two seemingly delicate gothic-kish bracelets concealing a lethal blade each, her chances against Cyrus in a direct confrontation were slim without a weapon. While some might call it cheating, she saw it as basic survival instinct. Eve pulled a light grunt of discomfort when her top brushed the cut on her breast, but the stitches would thankfully hold long enough. She grabbed her zip hoodie to hide her bracelets, guessing the total warrior look may send the message here-to-kill-you a bit too obvious.

"Long enough to do what?" she mumbled. "Kill the freaking giant?"

I kind of like him.

Armed and ready for any confrontation, she made her way through the maze of Cyrus's mansion, determined not to lose herself in its never-ending corridors, now that would look stupid. Eventually she reached the gym.

Cyrus was indeed pummelling an innocent sandbag with unrestrained intensity. Eve stood still, observing the raw power on display. Cyrus had stripped off his shirt, a sight that as usual woke up her primitive instincts. His multiple tattoos were moving in harmony with his muscles, covering most of his body, a sight she would never get tired of. Hopefully she was wrong, and he was just in a bad mood for no reason, and they would have passionate sex. Maybe they could even use his belt again. *A girl can hope, right?*

The powerful rhythm of his punches ceased when he finally spotted her from his corner. He turned to her, adjusting the bandages on his hands.

Eve walked towards him. "Why don't we cut the bullshit, and you tell me what's wrong?"

Cyrus snorted dismissively, cracking his knuckles with an air of defiance. "I know what you can do, I know what you do. I don't believe in the tiny innocent girl anymore."

"Because you seriously believed in it?" Eve retorted with a laugh. "We had sex in a fucking library for God's sake. And in a garage. And don't start me on with what you did to my poor butt this weekend."

Drawing closer to him, she moved sideways watching his every movement. Cyrus, however, remained motionless, his dark gaze tracking her every step.

"I had a look through your closet when you got attacked."

Eve froze. "Maybe you shouldn't have."

Why the hell didn't he say anything then?

Cyrus scoffed. "Oh I'm sorry, I was just trying to be helpful for my poor darling endangered girlfriend, packing some of your stuff so we could get out of that flat asap." He paused, watching her moving, she must look like a tiger ready to pounce, but really she was more of a kitten. "I hid everything when your colleagues arrived. I wasn't sure at first, I just thought that you had weird kinks."

"Well, to be fair, I do."

Cyrus chuckled. "Yeah that's what I like about you."

A heavy silence hung in the air.

"Do Ian and Zorfield know?" Eve's voice was barely above a whisper.

"Why? Are you gonna try to kill them too?"

"Only if you force my hand. I can't go to jail Cyrus, I am way too pretty for that." She didn't mention killing him would be a tenuous task, but if she had to go and deal with the couple, she would definitely not survive that.

Without warning, she lunged at him, but he was prepared, deftly throwing her aside, and she hit the ground as if she was a simple doll, but sprang back onto her feet in a heartbeat. He was much faster than he looked despite his size.

There was a relentless exchange of blows, each move calculated. Eve struggled to keep pace, her martial arts skills tested as she evaded most punches while attempting to land her own hits, but she was not a puncher, that's why she learned damn jiu-jitsu instead of freaking karate. He reach her face with his fist, which sent Eve to the ground, again, her head ringing. Getting the shit beat out of her was becoming a habit and she didn't enjoy it one bit. She got up quickly, her many talents wouldn't help her if he managed to stick her to the floor every damn time.

Eve breathed heavily, dazed. "I'm beginning to understand why everyone fears you."

"You haven't seen the half of it," Cyrus retorted, his eyes trained on her, his hands to his side but ready to jump.

"Nor have you." Eve smirked. "I'm sorry."

Cyrus looked at her, a question in his eyes, a sly smile appearing on his lips when Eve started taking off her hoodie, but he growled when she raised her wrists to her face, clenching both her knives.

"Come on Eve."

"Just so you know, I am perfectly aware this is cheating."

Kicks started again, faster and stronger, Eve heading for sensitive points, pretty excited to have found someone able to hold on to her. Cyrus was as stoic as usual, barely grunting when she finally reached his left arm with her knife. Eve held her breath at the few drops of blood now tainting the gym mat. Immediate remorse started eating her, but it was too late to stop.

Cyrus sniggered and jumped on her, accelerating his pace. She could feel the fatigue taking over, she was not used to this kind of fighting, her fights were usually short and sweet. *Maybe attacking Cyrus while on meds was not the smartest idea of the year.* She could totally see that now, but then she had been the Queen of Bad Decisions in the recent weeks.

Thinking about what losing would mean, she couldn't stop herself and glanced a dark look at Cyrus, accusing him of all her troubles.

Cyrus used the moment to drop and extend his leg in a basic hook, sending her straight to the ground. Again. The shock stunned her for a few seconds, and she tried to catch up her breath, but Cyrus rushed over, pinning her down with his massive frame. He secured her hands and weapons behind her back, her body contorted uncomfortably

Eve pouted, breathless "I shouldn't have cheated, should I?"

"Nope."

She sighed loudly. "Well, you won then, happy? I am still not going to jail. Just be quick."

Her lover's gaze remained searching, his stare piercing through her.

"Pretty please?" she added, trying to look the cutest she could.

"How exactly do you expect me to be happy about that Eve? You don't understand, do you? I DON'T CARE."

"I am a killer Cyrus, and you don't care? I am not a cute, accidental OMG-it-just-happened-killer. I hunt, I track, I torture, and I kill. And I LOVE it."

"I'm a killer too, no big deal, we all have our demons."

"You are talking about the war, I'm talking about my bloody hobby, I should be crocheting but instead I'm slashing dicks. I know you heard Erik on the boat, he was right you know…" her voice started breaking "I do like to kill, I can't stop Cyrus."

"So? You don't know anything about me yet my Goddess, I love killing too. The blood, the feeling of taking the life of some fucker who deserves it, or not. We enjoy the same things, but different. Think about it like we both love pizza, except you like pepperoni pizza and I prefer pineapple pizza."

Eve's eyes almost popped out of their sockets as she rolled them. "Monster"

Cyrus laughed loudly. "But you know what gets me? You were planning to leave without a word, weren't you? To vanish without giving us a chance. That you could even consider me and my friends as your enemies. We are on the same side," he said, speaking distinctly.

"We're not on the same side," Eve protested, her voice shaking.

Cyrus locked eyes with her, emphasising every word. "We. Are."

A heavy silence settled between them. Eve's mind raced, thoughts colliding.

"Anonymity matters," she argued, her voice a mere whisper. "You can't comprehend the bigger picture."

"I don't care about any bigger pictures, I only care about you. I have been taking care of the investigation on the 11's as well…Mark owes me a few favours."

He shifted her onto her belly despite her complaints, extracting her weapons and discarding them. Turning her back over, he drew her against him, holding her close. Eve winced as pain radiated from her wrists, still under the hard clench of her lover.

"I'm sincere, Eve. You're safe here. We'll protect you. I'll protect you. You're one of us. And if you have to go from time to time on a hunt, I am fine with it." He paused, his mouth twisted as if he was thinking hard about something. "Of course, I would rather not find any dicks on the breakfast table. Unless it's mine, still attached to my body, and ready to fuck you."

Eve's eyes rolled, not wanting to believe him, there was no such thing as a perfect boyfriend, was there?

"Zorf even started making you a friendship bracelet. Just give us a chance" he urged, a glimmer of a smile crossing his lips. "We'll forget about the throat-slitting attempt."

"Are you saying that because I kicked your ass?" Eve teased with a playful voice, inching a bit closer to him, moving her hips up and down the growing desire in Cyrus's pants.

"You don't look like you are in any position of kicking ass right now girl," Cyrus chuckled.

"Oh shut…"

Cyrus crashed his mouth onto hers, finally releasing her from his tight grip, with caution at first, the man observing her reaction with carefulness. She immediately moved her arms around his large shoulders, positioning him between her legs.

He looked at her again with an ironic air and slipped his hands under her tank top, pulling it up, plunging on her mouth for a kiss. He settled himself between Eve's welcoming legs, getting in a comfortable position, where he belonged. Her body finally let everything go, and while continuing to kiss and caress her, he pulled her top even more until finally removing it, paying extra attention not to touch her damaged breasts.

Quickly, he moved his body, contorting himself out of his sweatpants while Eve took care of hers, their eyes full of desire. The only thought Eve had was that she loved having his body glued to hers, no longer holding back her moan when she felt his finger creeping inside her, then two, deeper and deeper.

She clung to him like to a lifeline and in excitement whispered a vague "again" before he added a third, starting a rhythmic back and forth, stretching her drenched pussy, getting back to the old dance they knew so well.

On the verge of ecstasy, even faster than usual which was apparently a thing, Cyrus withdrew his fingers, earning him a grunt and a furious look that seemed to amuse him. Then, when she least expected it, he looked up, locked his eyes onto hers, pinned her wrists over her head, and in a violent thrust penetrated her.

181

Epilogue

Cyrus

Cyrus watched her, his Goddess, his Huntress, her long hair was tightly braided and bouncing to the rhythm of her wrist. Her wrist which was holding her new favourite knife, curtesy of Mr Perfect Boyfriend, and was busy slicing through this poor guy's guts.

"It should be forbidden to be so beautiful," he commented, a crystalline laughter answering him. His woman interrupted her bloody piece of art to quickly jump on him, surrounding his hips with her legs, catching his lips in a fiery kiss.

"I love you" she whispered.

Cyrus's eyes darkened at her words, his lust shining in those ocean eyes. He threw her on the table, and pulled up her dress, the view of her juicy cunt already drenched for him making him groan. Taking his hard dick out of its prison, he smiled.

"I love you too."

The End

Thank you

Thank you for reading and I hope you have enjoyed this story :) If you did, please consider writing a review on Amazon or Goodreads, it really does make a difference.

You can also find me on Instagram and Thread:
https://www.instagram.com/paulinewaltersauthor/
https://www.threads.net/@paulinewaltersauthor?hl=en

Do you want to know what's coming next? I also have a (pretty basic) website:
https://paulinewaltersauthor.com/

185